By Sherril Jaffe

BLACK SPARROW PRESS
SANTA ROSA 1991

SHERRIL JAFFE

HOUSE TOURS

Black Sparrow Press books are printed on acid-free paper.

Library of Congress Cataloging-in-Publication Data

Jaffe, Sherril, 1945-
  House tours / Sherril Jaffe.
    p. cm.
  ISBN 0-87685-862-0 (cloth : signed) : — ISBN 0-87685-861-2 (cloth) :
— ISBN 0-87685-860-4 (pbk.) :
  I. Title.
PS3560.A314H6   1991
813'.54—dc20
                          91-35730
                              CIP

for Virginia, Harriet, and Paula

"Architecture is fate."

HOUSE TOURS

I. A House Can Be Vindictive

I Was Walking

I WAS WALKING with my friend Virginia the other day. We like to take the dogs on the road through the woods down to a little house on the lake. Virginia says it's a good place to let the dogs run, but the real reason we go there is because we're attracted by the little house.

It's a tiny house and it sits right on the lake. Some of its rooms are cantilevered over the water; it reminds me of a houseboat. It has a stone fireplace and a tiny flagstone terrace. Someone has planted flowers in an old canoe next to it, and on one side there's a dock with a bench where you can sit and look out at the island. Twice I've seen a pair of blue herons there, but never any people. The people only come on weekends in the summer.

My husband won't go there because it's trespassing, but it doesn't feel that way to me. It feels like I am visiting the little house. Still, Virginia and I only go there on weekdays in the summer, but now that it's winter, and the lake is frozen and the little house is boarded up, we go there without worrying about being seen. Still, as we were climbing over some logs that had been dragged across the road and walking through the snow to the dock the other day, Virginia said, "I'm going to bring these people a little present next summer and tell them that we kept an eye on their house for them."

"That's right," I said. "We're doing them a favor by coming here. And besides, I'm sure the house gets very lonely in the winter and appreciates being visited."

"Ann," Virginia said, "houses don't have feelings."

"Of course they do," I said. "And I'm sure this house enjoys our visits."

"No, it doesn't," Virginia said.

We both looked at the house. It's very old and the roof goes up into a little cupola. Two windows flank the front door like eyes, but they have boards nailed over them now.

"Virginia," I said, "surely you've known a house to be angry. Houses can be very vindictive—when hurt. Surely you've had experience with a vindictive house." My own house in California had turned vindictive right before we moved and I knew what I was talking about.

"Yes, you're right," she said.

"So then, is it so far-fetched, since a house can feel angry, to think it could, alternately, feel lonely?"

We had walked to the middle of the little stone bridge that goes over the unnamed stream which runs into the lake on the other side of the little house. The stream was frozen, like the world just then, but just under the surface I could see that something was moving.

I Was Born

I WAS BORN IN a small town, Walla Walla, Washington. It was September of 1945, the end of the war, and my father was in the air force stationed there. Six months later, when his discharge came, we all, my mother, my father, my sister and I, drove to Los Angeles, where they all had been born and where they all always had lived until the war. Several years later, we were all on vacation at some national park. We were in a lodge. The rangers were doing a program for the children. The children were invited up on the stage. I stood next to my sister Barbara, and the ranger asked us where we were from. "Los Angeles," my sister said. For a moment, I was confused. I didn't know what to say. "Walla Walla," I said, trying to tell the truth.

Everyone was upset with me after that. I thought it was because it must be somehow shameful to come from such a place. For whatever reason, I knew I was different from the rest of them. I came from a different place.

I don't, of course, remember my home town, even though we returned there once on another family vacation. However, I feel the small town was somehow imprinted on my psyche, and I have lived in a series of similarly small towns since I grew up and left my parents' house, looking for home.

I Have Often Dreamed

I HAVE OFTEN DREAMED that I was in a house, a house that I had once lived in, or the house that I was then living in, or a house I was about to move into, and in my dream I discover that there are more rooms in the house than I knew were there. It is quite marvelous to discover all these new rooms and quite incredible that I never realized they were there, when, of course, they were there all along. It gives me a sense of expanding possibility, as when hiking down a narrow ravine to a creek at the bottom, when the creek becomes an estuary which gets wider and wider until suddenly it opens out into the wide sea. There is great joy in arriving there. I have been there, and made a fire on the rocks. The sea roars, and under my feet the round red stones are wet.

So it is in my dream—the house opens up, generous

and endless. These dreams are so real, that for a few moments after I wake I can still believe them, as reality closes in like walls.

My Parents Built

MY PARENTS ALWAYS BUILT their own houses because they didn't wish to live any place where anyone else had lived. They are true Californians and don't understand how I can love old houses.

The house they brought me to when we left Walla Walla was at 821 South Genesee, near Hancock Park in Los Angeles. It was white and later yellow with a shingled roof. There were door chimes and a front porch. Those same door chimes later appeared in the house I lived in in Sebastopol.

There was an entry hall and a crystal chandelier over the dining room table. I broke one of those crystals once batting a balloon around the room. The kitchen floor was linoleum, a red brick pattern which reappeared later in the log house I lived in outside of the town of Bloomfield. I saw this same linoleum the other day, in brown, on the floor of a house in a development in Central Valley, near where I live now.

The wallpaper in the room I shared with my sister on Genesee was rose chintz. It was darker over the heater where we would stand in the morning to get dressed. When I lay in bed the shapes and faces hidden in those flowers revealed themselves. The background came forward, and then was obliterated as night fell.

When I lived in Sebastopol, I had a lampshade made out of chintz fabric, and I hung it over the dining room table. We ate there on rose chintz dishes, and I brought those dishes with me when we moved east.

Last winter I found a rose chintz tray at the Metropolitan Museum gift shop. Every morning, now, I get up when it's still dark, and I go downstairs to make the coffee. Then I put it and the milk and a cup on this tray, and I bring it upstairs where my husband will find it when he wakes up after I have gone.

There Was a Den

THERE WAS A DEN WITH A CORNER fireplace in that house on
Genesee. It was knotty pine, and we spent a lot of time in
there watching t.v. and eating oranges. I sat in my father's lap.
    People don't have dens any more, they have family rooms.
When my parents built their house in Beverly Hills they
didn't build a den, they built a family room which was
separated from the living room only by a sliding shoji screen.
We sat in there and watched slides of the house going up.
There is one of me standing at the bottom of the pool when
it was just a hole in the ground with ribs of steel lining the
dirt.
    But for all I know, people don't have family rooms
anymore, either, they have something else. The other day
I had a shock when I visited at the house of an acquaintance.
The house is in a development, and has a living room, dining room, kitchen and family room on the first level. Her

husband has recently switched jobs and started a limousine service, so they have purchased two stretch limos. When I stepped into their house I noticed something was different. Their family room was missing. It has been walled off and made into a garage to house the limos.

I rode in one of their limousines once. There is everything you could possibly want in there—comfortable upholstery, a telephone, a full bar, a refrigerator, and a t.v. with a VCR.

We Have Decided

WE HAVE DECIDED TO BUY THE house we have been renting. The price isn't particularly high, but we will still be paying more than half again each month in payments. However, my husband is due to get a raise in August, and this will offset the expense to some extent, and also there will be a tax benefit.

Several people who know our situation have asked us why we don't simply continue renting, but I have explained that I am really anxious to make some improvements on the house. We have been living there a year and a half, and I know exactly what needs to be done. These improvements aren't major, but they'll make a big difference in our level of comfort.

"You know," several people have suggested, "you can still make these improvements while renting. It will still cost you less a year for housing."

"But do you think the landlord would let us?" I asked.

"Why not?" several people have said. "It would be to his advantage to have the property improved. But you'd have to get a good lease. A five-year lease."

"A five-year lease?" I asked. "I don't know if we're going to be here that long. My husband's contract runs out in two years. There's a good chance it will be renewed, but anything can happen."

What I meant by "anything can happen" is that I'm not sure my husband will want to stay in his job after two years. It is entirely possible that he will take a job in another part of the country. We have moved before.

It is true that we all like it here, and a lot of the time my husband feels fulfilled in his work. Then there are those days and months of despair, when my husband feels he is failing, when he thinks he's not doing any good here and should go somewhere else.

During these periods I am utterly at sea. This house which I usually love so well, and which I feel our family is quite perfectly suited to, begins to fall apart as I look at it. It becomes a mockery, a joke of a house. Then I see how foolish it would be to buy this house, if we are just going to sell it two years down the road. But it's also foolish for us to live for even those two years without the conveniences we desire. We can rent the house with a two-year lease, put in the conveniences, and when we leave, we will have saved money and the landlord will be left with a better house. Let him have it.

No, I can't do it. At first it seemed like a good idea. I felt relieved, rescued from making a foolish commitment. But right now my husband seems fulfilled in his work. If we just got a two-year lease it would mean that we thought we probably weren't going to stay here forever. How long would my husband be able to remain fulfilled if he couldn't believe that this place was the place that was meant for him to be, to do the work that only he can do, if he had to think that this was just the place where he was stuck for two years before he could go on to the place he was meant to be?

That is why we have decided to buy this house instead of renting it. We know that death will claim us someday, but we have to pretend it's not true.

Most of the Time

Most of the time when i walk the dog I go out the front door and down to the lake. We walk along the shore until the road takes us up a hill. We follow that road until it ends in another which takes us back down to the lake again. Then we follow the shore until that road takes us back up the hill to our house, and we go back in the front door.

But sometimes we continue on beyond the house and up around another block so that we approach the house from the side. I call this "sneaking up on the house," and once, when walking with a friend, I took her this way and told her that was what we were doing. Then I began tip-toeing down the road as the side of the house came into view, as if I really were trying to take it by surprise.

Of course, when I did this, I was really joking. I had no intention of actually scaring my house. I was only reflecting what the house does to me when I came across it from the side.

From the front, the house is quite simple. Two sash windows flank the front door, and four second story bedroom windows are aligned over them. Three steps go up to a stone porch held by giant rhododendron bushes. There is a glassed-in porch on one side and a portico over the front door. A large dogwood and two flowering cherries shield the house from the eyes of the street.

The house is on a corner, on a double lot, and when you come across it from the side, you see it necessarily from a distance. It stands on a hill, and is quite tall. You have to look up to see it, and it is so pleasing to gaze upon with its windows opening on so many different levels, that I am always startled. That is partly the reason that I tip-toe down the street as it comes into view.

The house is a Dutch colonial revival, probably built around 1910. It is white with green trim, and has what is called a side gambrel roof. The roof pitches down from the peak in both directions, then pitches again at another angle before meeting the wall. There is something very comforting about the shape of this roof. It's like shoulders.

When I sneak up on the house from the side, I mean that when I come across the house in this unexpected way it always sneaks up on me and takes me by surprise. I tip-toe because I like to slow down and savor the effect.

Last Friday morning my husband returned after being away at a conference all week. I was upstairs when I heard his car, and saw him coming in through the side door when I reached the landing on the stairs. I saw him as if I'd never seen him before, his boyish crop of hair, his triangular eyebrows, his sweet shy smile, the cleft in his strong chin. There were little lines around his eyes. Had he had trouble sleeping alone, as I had when he was gone? His eyes were glowing. I could sense his full open heart as he set down his suitcase and I came down the stairs, and he took me in his arms.

His taste was sweet, though his lips were cool, reminding me how cold was the world outside.

I Received

I RECEIVED IN THE MAIL THE other day the opportunity to participate in the Publisher's Weekly sweepstakes. It was a packet filled with stickers and information. The stickers were each miniature versions of all the magazines they are selling which you can subscribe to simply by tearing out and sticking on the entry form. This I didn't do, as I hate reading magazines. They remind me of going to the dentist's office. "Of course, you don't have to subscribe to any magazines to win, Mrs. A. Golden," another enclosure said, "but unless you start subscribing to some magazines soon we may not be able to send you any more entry forms to our sweepstakes."

"But if you won the sweepstake, your life would be meaningless," I said to the hygienist at the dentist's office.

There was a sticker amongst the other stickers that one could punch out if one specifically wanted to win a Jaguar. You could choose which color you wanted, and stick that sticker on the Jaguar. It was just about like picking out a car in the showroom.

However, I don't actually believe I'm going to win a Jaguar, so it was safe for me to mail in my entry. My parents did once win a Ford Thunderbird, so I know it's not impossible. Maybe they wouldn't have picked that particular car, but they drove it for years, and when it finally gave out they got a new one. They must have felt that God wanted them to have a Thunderbird, the way my husband and I feel God must have wanted us to live in this house, because, after all, He dumped us here.

The strangest item in the sweepstakes packet, however, is the picture of the dream house which one will be able to buy if one wins the sweepstakes. We are inside the entry of the house. To the right is the doorway to another room. The house must be very old, because doors aren't framed so heavily anymore. There are several coats of paint on the molding, and it's just a matter of time before some of this paint begins to crack and chip off, or hang in loose wafers. I can see into the kitchen. It seems very dark and I don't think it's been remodeled for many years. It's yellow. I can see part of the metal legs of a kitchen table from the sixties.

However, from where I'm standing I can choose to look up the wide staircase, though I can't see where it leads. Someone has placed tulips in a vase in a niche part way up. The staircase is wooden, but carpeted with a red runner with gold stripes going down each edge. It's the kind of carpet that kings walk on in stories.

It's Good

IT'S GOOD THAT I SAID THAT we have decided to buy the house, because that enabled me to see that I certainly don't want to buy the house at all, but just to continue renting it. I only wanted to buy it out of some deep sentimentality, some obeisance to the American dream, so much tied up with ownership and mortgages. Two more sweepstake opportunities have arrived in the mail, each with its own version of a dream house.

One was for a vacation house. It was all angles, sharp and without any particular design—but large. The other was nondescript except for some enormous concrete tubular protrusions. I cannot understand why these monstrosities are advertised as dreamhouses one will be able to buy after winning the sweepstake. Can it be that the average impoverished person has never seen a beautiful house, so will accept these images as dreams worth subscribing to magazines for?

What really changed my mind about ownership was a plumber who had been recommended to me by a successful businessman. I asked him to come over and inspect the boiler. The boiler is extremely old, and was originally designed for coal. It was then converted for use with oil, and there is a large tank half filled with oil next to it in the basement. But finally it was converted to natural gas. I wanted to know if it was going to need replacing.

The day the plumber came was grey and muddy with melting snow. It was not that he was a particularly large man, but there was something about him that made the house shrink as soon as he came in the door. My dog wouldn't stop jumping on him, and I couldn't stop bumping into him as I led him through the living room, now so small that we were across it in one stride, through the diminutive dining room and the kitchen, which was now the size of a postage stamp, to the basement stairs, bumping into each other and trying to disengage ourselves from the dog.

We stood there, then, for several minutes, by the boiler in the dilapidated basement, while he explained what big jobs he has done, how he installed sinks that cost $900 apiece into enormous houses, and I realized that the basement was nothing but a bad dream.

One day I was doing the laundry down there and I looked up at the hot water pipes right by my head and I saw this white insulation ripped and hanging down—asbestos! Suddenly I saw all the pipes covered in this stuff and it all coming apart and polluting my world. Then the sky out the window opened up, and I saw clearly how the whole earth was polluted and how hopeless everything is. We are doomed.

After that I got a repair man to cover and seal the stuff, and I repressed that vision so that I could only see it in my dreams.

I asked the plumber about this or that project, but he had

no enthusiasm for my ideas. They would all require cutting big holes, he said. It would be better if he could put them in a house without furniture and without people.

We Were Very Lucky

WE WERE VERY LUCKY TO GET an apartment in Manhattan when my husband was in school. It was in a building owned by Columbia University. A cousin's boyfriend was teaching there and he rented it for us. My mother-in-law had the floors sanded and poly-urethaned before we came, and the bathroom and kitchen were redone. The whole place was freshly painted white. The first day I walked around the empty rooms I looked up and saw something crawling way up on the ceiling. "Is that a roach?" I asked. I had always lived in California and had never seen a cockroach before. "No," the super said. "It couldn't be."

I learned never to go into the kitchen there at night. I didn't want to turn on the light and see the roaches scuttling away. I didn't want to call the exterminator because I had two little children and I didn't want the whole apartment polluted with poison. Roaches, after all, don't carry disease.

And besides, extermination doesn't last very long since the roaches come up from the apartment downstairs and come down from the apartment upstairs. Several times I even saw roaches crawling in under the front door. The front door didn't quite meet the floor. It was made out of a heavy metal and had replaced the original wooden door as part of the remodeling. Every time it closed, it slammed, and part of the molding in the hallway would fall off.

What was worse than the roaches, however, were the mice. Every time my husband went into a final exam period the pressure would mount and mice would start coming out of the woodwork. Usually I would dream of a nest of mice before I would actually see them. I could never decide whether these were prophetic dreams or whether I had somehow glimpsed the mouse in the peripheries of my vision without registering it consciously.

That was one of the horrifying things about them—that they moved in the peripheries of my vision down the wall under the cabinets in the kitchen, that I would see them without seeing them.

"They're cute," my husband would say, but they disgusted and terrified me. When I saw one I would grab the babies and run into the living room, my older one screaming "Mouse! Mouse!" Then I would get on the phone and call the library at my husband's school to have him paged.

That apartment had a long narrow hall. I parked my double stroller in it. There were two small bedrooms at the end, where the girls slept, then the bathroom, then the kitchen, and then an interior room with a window on the court, which we used as a living-dining room. This was separated by sliding doors from a room fronting on the street, where my husband and I slept. Off of this was also a tiny study. The ceilings were very high, and the windows were tall and large. We were five floors up, and I never felt claustrophobic there, but periodically bongos or screams of agony would well up from the court. I always worried about the effect of these sounds on my babies, and my toddler, although not, like me, afraid of mice, was afraid of things she couldn't see, and called me every night down the long dark hall that separated us.

I wasn't working at the time, and spent most of my day alone in the apartment with the babies, and there were countless days, between mouse-attacks, that the three of us played on the floor in the back bedroom, the sun shining in through the tall casement window. Other days we sat on my bed, where I nursed the baby and read them a story. Sometimes we were just quiet, and gazed out the window.

We were very lucky that just across the street there was a gap between the buildings for a parking lot. In front of it was a tree. But more wonderful than that was all the sky we could see. And most beautiful of all were the water towers, dark red and gray, on the roof of a building a block away.

I Am Trying

I AM TRYING TO RECONSTRUCT the floor plan of the house on Genesee, but there are certain aspects of it I can't piece together. How, for example, did one get into the den? Was it directly from the dining room, or the hall, which must have started in the dining room, if not in the front hall. There was a door leading out of the den to the patio, I know, and there must have been another leading into the back porch. The dining room led into the kitchen with a swinging door and was connected to the front hall by an arch. There was another door, perhaps, which led into the den, or the back hall. Could all these rooms have so many doors?

The bedroom I shared with my sister had a door leading to the hall which ended at my parents' room. My parents left the light on in the hall for me at night, and I lay in bed looking at it, until the light broke into separate motes. My bed was pushed against another door, which led to the entry hall.

Why was there a door leading into the entry hall from that room? The entry hall had three doors, then, including the front door and the front hall closet door, and two arches, one to the living room and the other to the dining room. It was a heart, with veins going into it and arteries going out.

The floor plan of this house, where I lived from the age of six months until I was eleven, is my genetic code. I am trying to crack it. Somewhere in it is the explanation for all of my traits. It is the map of my particularity. If only I could reconstruct it I might at last begin to understand my life.

Once, on a visit to my parents' house in Los Angeles, we drove past the house on Genesee. But we got lost getting there. It was not easy to find. The street had been changed from a straight street to a curved one, from a link between perpendicular larger streets, to a twisted cul-de-sac.

The house was white again, and there were bars on the windows.

We Went to Visit

WE WENT TO VISIT SOME FRIENDS today who are Holocaust survivors. Really we went to see their house. For many years, they have been coming to this house on weekends, but now they are retiring, and they want to live here permanently. The problem is, this house is too small to accomodate all of their things from the city. So they are debating back and forth about whether they should put additions on this house or buy another, larger house. They have been talking with architects and going around with real estate agents. But they still can't make up their minds. They are very attached to this house, but it is just too small for them.

We found the house on a busy road. When we stood by the front door we could hear cars going by.

"When we first moved here," they said, "this was just a back road. Now it's a major thoroughfare."

The front room had a dark floor. There was a white fluffy

rug on it in front of the fireplace. "I had always dreamed of having a dark wood floor with a white bearskin rug on top of it," my friend said. "This isn't bearskin, but it's furry. We used to lie here all the time in front of the fire. But not so much anymore."

They led us into a sun room, an enclosed porch with skylights. "I wanted a room where I could be inside, but it would be like being outside," my friend explained. Through the windows we could see the above-ground pool in the neighbor's yard. "They just cut down a whole bunch of trees," they said. "We never could see that thing before."

They led us out the back and across the yard to their own in-ground pool, covered with black plastic now. "I didn't want to see the pool from the house," my friend explained. "In the summer, when the leaves are on the trees, you can't see any of these houses," she said, gesturing around.

We stopped on our way back to the house to replace a stone that had fallen out of the little wall that surrounded a rhododendron bush. But it fell out again.

Back in the house, we went to look at the bedrooms which were up a small flight of stairs. "This was Mama's room," my friend said, when we entered the last bedroom. "She did all the needlepoint," she said. On the walls were several small needlepoint pictures.

"Mama died two days after we moved here," my friend's husband said later, when we were back in the sun room having coffee.

"I don't see how you can move from here," I said.

"Another architect's coming tomorrow," my friend said.

They showed us to the door and helped me on with my coat. I turned to say goodbye and to thank them. They were standing framed in the doorway. Over their heads was a large crack in the plaster.

I Have Been

I HAVE BEEN TRYING TO STRAIGHTEN up the house a little so I can get down to work. I threw away the junk mail lying on the table and made the beds. I gathered the laundry and took some to the basement. Then there are these other things—this postcard from a friend who is living abroad, which I will also throw away, and this pile of school work my little daughter left in the car which I would like to keep, because she put her hand to it. And so I put it in a file with her name on it on a shelf by my desk. From there it will go into a bag in the attic, and someday that bag will be sorted through. A few striking items will be removed and the rest will be discarded.

Right now I know I have to go through everything in the attic and reorganize it. I must give or throw most of it away. It is getting difficult to even walk up the attic stairs. Even the steps are piled high with things.

Part of the reason for this is that most of the attic is stuffed

41

with the landlord's things, the things that were in the house when we decided to rent it.

When we first looked at the house it had been closed up for several years. It had been used as a summer house for a family who lived in the city. Then, suddenly, the mother died.

The children were now married, and then the father remarried, and no one came back to the house to look at the things which had been left there. There were heavy drapes on the windows, and light curtains behind these, and behind these there were shades.

It was the only house for rent in that area at the time we were looking. I opened the drapes and pulled back the curtains. Then I raised the shades. Light came into the room and landed on all the knicknacks. There was a pipe in an ashtray. There was laundry in the dryer. Every drawer was full of things. "We'll take it," I said. Movers came and put all the things in the attic.

I felt sorry for the woman who had died, the woman who had had a relationship with each of these objects. But what can be done with all of the things which pertain to an individual life?

I remember going with my mother-in-law to go through the things in her mother's apartment after she had died. She thought I might be able to use some of the things, and I did take two green corduroy comforters. My girls used them for many years, until they began to fray and then to dissolve faster than I could mend them. Now the remnants of them are in the attic.

I also took a kind of fifties tablecloth from a pile of neatly folded, starched and ironed cloths, most of which had spots.

There were also drawers of costume jewelry, ropes of pearls and beads, which I didn't touch. From the kitchen I took a device for opening hard to open jars, and I still use this. But nothing else.

My friend the real estate agent took me to look at houses

the other week so that I could be sure I wanted to live where I did. On the day we rented our house we thought it would just be temporary. But we have refused to move. We feel we were brought here for a reason. But other times it seems like it must be some terrible mistake. And so I went with my friend to look at other houses.

The people weren't at home in most of the houses he showed me. Most of the houses he showed me were very large, and all the rooms were filled with furniture.

He led me up to the second story of a blue house and into each bedroom, opening each closet door to show me, and each closet was filled with things. "And now, wait till you see what's behind this door," he said, when we entered the third bedroom. Behind that door was a huge unheated attic space which stretched over the garage. "Look at this storage space!" my friend said. In there, on racks, in boxes, piled to the ceiling, were more things, the cumulative dross of the lives of the people who lived in the blue house and wanted to move.

I Am Sitting

I AM SITTING IN THE DINING room of the piano teacher's Victorian house while my children take lessons. We are usually cold here, and I keep my coat on. We come directly from their art lessons which they come to directly from school, so they always need to use the bathroom, and I must always go with them upstairs, where it is dark, turning on the lights for them and standing by the door for them.

The bathroom is large and pink with flowered wall paper and a wooden floor. There are sea shells in a little niche by the tub. Once, one of my daughters opened the second door in there, which I thought connected with a bedroom, and revealed a large closet full of things.

Before we go back downstairs we glance into the bedroom and the stairs leading to the third floor. None of the furniture matches, and a lot of it is quite old. However, the plants are all healthy and good looking. Many of them are lined up on a cloth spread over the radiator under the window in the dining room. No wonder it is so cold in here—they don't use the heat.

Nevertheless, I don't mind coming here or waiting while they each take a lesson. I am just happy that my girls are getting piano lessons at last. We put it off for a number of years while we lived in the city and knew we would be moving because we didn't want to buy a piano and move it twice.

Now my big girl is playing "Ode to Joy," a piece I remember playing when I had lessons when I was a little girl. In those days, piano teachers, like doctors, came to your house. I remember sitting at the black piano with the word "Baldwin" written over the keyboard. Mr. Bridenstein was coming to give my sister and me our lessons.

Mr. Bridenstein was at the door. "Oh, Mr. Bridenstein," I said. "There's something I want to show you!"

My parents had recently completed some remodeling in the house. They had remodeled the pink bathroom my sister and I shared. I led him to the door and opened it. There was my sister, sitting on the toilet.

To this day, she has not forgiven me for this. That was the end of our piano lessons. I don't know why my mother didn't simply get us another teacher. Only now, taking my girls for their lesson, am I following through. I can see through the lace curtains of the living room into the night, where a red sign which says "Mobil" turns and turns.

From the Window

FROM THE WINDOW OF MY HOUSE in Sebastopol I could see mountains. These were blue, then purple as the light faded and night came on. One of these was shaped like a volcano, Mt. St. Helena, where Robert Louis Stevenson once lived and got the landscape he used in *Treasure Island*. Even though these mountains were sixty miles north, on clear cold days we could see the plumes of the geysers rising from them.

When the rains came, the valley flooded, and beneath the window spread a giant grey lake with tree-tops sticking out of it. In the summer, the leaves of these trees shimmered in the wind, and the trees receded backwards into a dark green shadow. It was beautiful, yet it was sad, as windows that face north inevitably are.

We had an oddly similar view from our window the year we lived in Jerusalem. But this time we looked east, across the desert to the hills of Moab, and in the center of the view was Herodian, another volcano-shaped mountain. We had come there after our cousin's boyfriend had lost his job at Columbia, after we had lost the Columbia apartment. The air was as pure as the sun rising, and we would have stayed there had not someone else found another apartment in Manhattan for us.

It was on the upper west side, near my husband's school, where we needed to be. My mother-in-law had the floors sanded for us before we came, and it was freshly painted white. It was much larger than our other New York apartment, even though there were fewer rooms. The ceilings were very high and the windows very tall. They were new, and I could tip them inward to wash them on the outside.

The view from the back bedroom where our girls slept in bunk beds was of the windows in the building next door. Our apartment was on the tenth floor and that building was ten stories high, so we could see the sky hanging over it. Three large windows in the living room looked across the street at the ornate facade of another grey building. Sometimes we could see a cat walking across a ledge ten stories up, and sometimes people, sitting at their desks or exercising in their rooms. From half of our living room, and from the master bedroom, we could see the edge of that building, where it broke off into space, and beyond it, down below, the tufted tops of the trees in Central Park. The park was even more in view from the window of the room where my husband and I slept, and we could lie in bed when they were performing the *1812* Overture there and watch the fireworks exploding over the dark trees without hearing the music.

Most of all I liked to lie on the couch or in my bed and look up at the scroll work which overhung the windows with the sky diffused beyond it. When I sat up, however, I saw the other buildings, with other windows looking back at me. There was no where I could sit without imagining I was being watched.

I wandered from room to room, sitting and looking out. However, in no spot was I entirely comfortable until I made a nook for myself with bookcases in the very center of the apartment. Now when I sat down I was protected on all sides, and there I sat with my face to the wall. I sat with my face to the wall and I turned my gaze inward.

My First Husband

MY FIRST HUSBAND AND I BOUGHT the house in Sebastopol from his best friend, John Hatfield, who had gone to South Africa to teach in a university. We had been married two years before in the log house some miles west, up on English Hill. I didn't want to leave that hill, but the night before we moved I dreamed that I discovered more rooms in the house in Sebastopol than I knew were there, and when we came, I removed all the curtains from the windows. There was no one to look in, and the house opened up. However, I had to put heavy drapes over the windows in the bedroom as my husband always stayed up at night and slept most of the morning. I always had to get up in the dark and feel my way quietly out of the room, because he would become angry if I woke him by mistake. Our marriage was bad, but I couldn't see it.

The house was rather hodge-podge. It had been built by

a Mr. Jewett who had lived there until his death. He must have been a fanciful character, because he put up an odd weathervane made out of a piece of blown glass over the driveway and set marbles in cement in front of the back door. He also built a cement bird-bath in the rose garden. I think he must have used an inner tube as the form. Water from the kitchen came down in the second level of the terraced garden, watering it, instead of going into the septic tank. It poured out of a hole that reminded me of miniature golf. There is a house with a similar arrangement two streets from here, and often, when I'm walking the dog, we see the water pouring across the road.

Mr. Jewett also made a wall out of home-made cement blocks which held up the orchard which rose on the other side of the driveway. These blocks were decorated with marbles, abalone shells and bottles, much like Watts Towers. But one day there was a terrible rainstorm. I was at work when it started. I had to drive across the plain to get home, and I was just coming up the drive, congratulating myself on arriving safely, when I saw the wall.

There was something funny about the wall. The wall was not there.

There had been a mudslide, and it had pushed the wall over. That is one explanation. The other is that the house was trying to get my attention, to let me know that things were not as they should be.

I was very upset at first. The wall was a piece of folk art. It was a conversation piece. But gradually, the rain stopped. A backhoe came and leveled out the hill a bit. Wildflowers grew on the bank. And eventually I came to see that the hill felt better without the wall.

With the Help of a Friend

With the help of a friend, another glamorous female, I attempted to distract the man, the large powerful man. But we could not seduce him away from his mission. She fell away, and so I attached myself to him on the stairs, offering my body, though he was a brute, stupid, with small eyes and calloused hands, but he was not interested, he would make his way down. Once in the basement, he went directly to the place I feared the most, the place where the basement was most unfinished, where it dissolved into soil, and there he began to dig, with a stick, with a spoon, with his bare hands, as if he knew what he was after, as if he knew what was hidden there, until he found them there, the bones, the human bones, which, I realized then, I myself had hidden. I had committed some unspeakable horror and buried the remains here, down in the basement under my house, so deep that the memory was lost, until the blind force came and found the dry white bones.

I Am Inside

I AM INSIDE. OUTSIDE, THE rain falls, bringing on the spring. I am an animal in a hollow tree. I can hear the rain against the bark, calling out the buds. Inside, everything is in order. Spring will come. The world is going to continue.

I'm tired after a long winter, living in my space capsule with the black void sucking at the glass, with the frozen dry hush on the world. Now that the grass beneath the windows is pushing upward, I would like to sleep, the house holding me in its arms, cradling me in the grey day. Then the house adjusts its breathing to mine and fills me up with dreams.

The Architect Who Designed

THE ARCHITECT WHO DESIGNED my parents' house in Beverly Hills had a challenge in placing the house on a lot which had a lot of hill and very little flat space. The lot had been a lucky find. Because of its size and shape it was not very expensive, despite its location. My mother found it. She very much wanted to move away from our house on Genesee, where she saw the neighborhood changing, to Beverly Hills, where the schools were better.

My father, on the other hand, wanted to stay in that house on Genesee forever, and he offered to buy my mother's half. Nevertheless, she prevailed. The house on Genesee was painted yellow so that it would sell quicker, the architect was engaged, and the lot was graded.

My sister and I were very excited about moving. We would at last get our own rooms, and, more important, we were going to get a swimming pool. We were not too young, either, to be unaware of the value of a Beverly Hills address.

The architect was a man my father knew through his business—Joe Jordan. He made a model of the house before it was built. The site was at the end of a private road which ran beneath the street. When you climb the hill now to get the mail you can see the house the way it looked in the model. It has pink rocks on the roof, but from above, these only appear to be tiny pebbles.

There is a breezeway between the carport and the house, full of plants, and the plants were there in the model, tiny and spongy. I loved this little house, but it frustrated me that I couldn't see inside to the rooms.

The house had many futuristic devices. There was an intercom through which you could communicate with any other room and even speak with people out at the pool. My father woke me every morning with this device. His amplified voice would break into my room and roust me from my bed. My parents also had a control panel by their bed from which the lights could be turned on or off in other parts of the house. They could push one of the buttons and start the coffee in the morning. They could see if they had left a light on the back of the house when they went to bed, and turn it off without actually having to go back there. If my sister or I got up in the middle of the night for a snack, a red light would be illuminated next to my mother, and she would come bursting through her door. We learned to feel our way around the kitchen and to stand in the light cast by the open refrigerator door.

Our parents' room was in a different zone from ours. Our rooms were in the back. They were small, because of the restrictions of the lot. Mine was actually cantilevered over the gully, and my sister's was opposite the kitchen. We had sliding doors to save space, and they rattled hollowly when we slid them into the wall. Sometimes at night I would hear my sister's door rattle as she felt her way into the kitchen.

My room was actually opposite the laundry, and I was usually awakened by the sound of the machines. Because of this situation, perhaps, what I longed for most in life was privacy, and I developed a reputation in the family for being secretive.

My parents' suite of rooms was clear on the other side of the house, behind a heavy door which closed automatically. Joe Jordan must have thought that teenagers, as we were getting to be, were noisy, and parents needed some escape from them. My parents' bedroom was large, with a sliding glass door that went out to the yard. They had a bathroom, a dressing room, a study, and a large walk-in closet that was always kept locked.

I wished when they built the house that they would put in a secret staircase or a secret room or, at the very least, a secret drawer, but they didn't. My desk was built into the wall, as were my shelves and my drawers. There was no way I could rearrange my room.

I had a large window which looked out at the gully. The house was built on a slab, and the floor was at ground level. When the gardeners or the pool men were outside I closed my curtain, and I listened to their boots crunching on the pink gravel path beneath my window. I was afraid they would see me. This window didn't open, but at one end was a louver which I could roll open. When I wanted air, I would turn the crank, and air would come through the slats.

I Didn't Really Know

I DIDN'T REALLY KNOW ABOUT developments until I moved to this area whre most people live in them. In California, they are known as tract houses. These are the houses the roofs of which we would see peeking over the top of a wall as we drove along the freeway.

There were no tract houses in Beverly Hills, of course, but when I was a junior in high school I had a boyfriend who lived over the hill, in Reseda, and he lived in one of them. He took me there once.

I was disapointed to discover that his house was not so very different from my parents'. There were beam ceilings and sliding glass doors. If I didn't come from a higher social class than this boy, then I had no idea what his interest in me could be.

Still I knew, even if it wasn't immediately obvious, that there were subtle differences between our houses. After all, ours had been on the cover of the home section of the Sunday *Los Angeles Times.* The stones in the fireplace had been hauled in from Utah. The frame had been especially treated to resist termites. There was something about that tract house that scared me. It looked like my parents' house, but I sensed there was something unwholesome about it.

Teenagers from all over his neighborhood came and went in his house. I had only one friend in my own neighborhood, Laura, and the Beverly Hills police would stop us to ask us our business when we walked each other home.

My boyfriend's parents were divorced, and he lived in that tract house with his mother, his stepfather and his stepsister. His stepsister was about his age, and not unattractive. I came out of the bathroom and saw them kissing on the bed.

Later, When I Grew Up

LATER, WHEN I GREW UP, AND moved to the log house on English
Hill, Laura said, "This looks just like your parents' house."
There was a stone fireplace and there were beam ceilings and
there was a lot of glass. "Do you really think so?" I asked,
full of hope. We were cleaning the house in preparation for
my wedding. I was about to marry the man I had been living
with in secret so that my parents would think that I was
respectable.

Of course, my parents didn't see it that way. They never
approved of that house because it was out in the middle
of nowhere. And it didn't really look much like their house,
either. It was made out of logs, notched together. The inside
walls were the same as the outside walls. There was no
plate glass like at my parents' house. The large window
in the living room was broken into small panes, each fram-
ing the view.

It looked west. Through this window I could see past the dark cypresses that stood in front of the house almost to the sea, eight miles away. Each afternoon in the summer I watched the giant bank of fog rise above the water and march forward to engulf the western hills. As it came towards me, the wind picked up, preceding it, and then swiftly it was upon me, surrounding the house and filling the windows with grey light.

It had been blazing hot at noon. The mallow with their pale blossoms were waist high, and I had waded through them to the abandoned orchard with its wooden knotted apples. I thought, then that I was in the garden of Eden.

But the winter storms also came from the west. The window buckled in the wind and the rain streamed in. There was nothing to protect the little house but the stone fireplace. I tried to keep the fire stoked, but the rain seeped through the porous rocks above the hearth, and tears appeared above the flames.

I Am Fond of Getting Up

I AM FOND OF GETTING UP IN the dark. I come downstairs and sit in my tape-back rocker facing south, and facing east. Upstairs, everyone sleeps. The windows are black squares. Then the dawn comes—pink, and orange, and ultimately, blue.

I don't have any memory of dawn at all as a child. Dawn comes slowly in California. There is usually fog in the morning, and by the time it burns off the sun is already high in the sky.

When I first met my husband, the man who was to be the father of my children, he was living in a cottage in Berkeley. It was small, and quite humble, but it made me love him. He had put straw mats on the floor and a lace curtain on the window. He had a table painted yellow and a straw chair. There was a guitar on the wall and a bathtub on legs.

I awakened in his house just as the fog burned off. I could

61

hear the water running in the big white tub. I rose and stood barefoot on the soft straw mat, pulling his robe around me, and the house filled up with yellow light.

We Took That Bathtub

WE TOOK THAT BATHTUB ON LEGS from his cottage to my house in Sebastopol. We had bought my first husband's half.

As soon as my first husband left I took down all the mirrors in the house. I opened all the doors and windows so that the house could breath, and I rearranged all the furniture. Now my new love and I put his bathtub up in the dormer window overlooking the orchard. We needed to rent out the attic in order to make the payments on the house.

We put an eight foot long skylight in the ceiling up there, and the light came into the long room. We hoped that someday we would have the whole house to ourselves, that we would be able to sit in that tub and watch the apples ripen. But it was not to be. We only lived there three years before we moved to New York.

There were many other things I wanted to do to that house that we never got around to. John Hatfield had covered the linoleum in the kitchen with a blue and green shag rug. This, of course, looked very strange, and I never felt I could get it clean. He also put green and white striped paper on the walls above the half-walls of fake pale blue tile that Mr. Jewett must have thought was a good idea. I never got used to these things, they always bothered me, but we never had any money leftover from our other projects in the house during the time we were there to do anything about them.

There are many things, also, I would like to change in this house, where I am currently living. I would like to paint the paneling white and remove the fake tile from the floor. Mr. Friedman, who owns this house, must have thought it was a good idea. But most of all, I would like to put a bathtub in. There is only a shower.

When we first moved here, I used to think about doing these things a lot. I even went so far as to get estimates. But somehow I know they will never get done. There are other projects in the house which are taking precedence, and I don't know how much longer we will be here, anyway.

My First Husband's Best Friend

MY FIRST HUSBAND'S BEST FRIEND, John Hatfield, returned to Sebastopol after he lost his job in South Africa. He had been arrested for drunk driving. He had no reason for being in Sebastopol, but nowhere else to be. He had been raised on a farm in Victoria, B.C., where his brother, an Anglican minister, still lived, but John was an alcoholic and a homosexual, and he couldn't go back there. Since we were living in his house, he bought another house down in a swampy area nearby.

It had shingles on the inside walls. He furnished it with camel hassocks which he had gotten in Africa and a large color t.v., and he set about digging up the trees and moving them to different places on the property. He acquired a small dog and a lame turkey which followed him around. This later drowned in a rainstorm and lay unburied in the yard.

An old cowboy named Tiny moved into a little shed at

the end of the garden where the back pasture began. He helped John to buy sickly calves at auction, which they fed with bottles out in the falling-down barn. But they died anyway. At night Tiny helped John to drink himself insensible. A long extension cord gave Tiny power from the main house.

I don't know what became of Tiny when John sold that house and moved to Graton, a depressed farm community nearby which was full of displaced Mexicans. Maybe moving was the only way John could get away from Tiny.

John had a mania for redecorating and home improvement. He began to paint the walls red and orange, and some had stripes, so there was a circus effect. Then small Mexican boys and lines of empty liquor bottles began to appear in the living room.

When he died, I didn't go to the funeral. By that time I had disengaged myself from my bad marriage and all its excess baggage. But I heard he had a sliding glass door put into the dining room wall. It was on the second story, and one day he slid open that door and stepped out.

I Had a Job

I HAD A JOB TEACHING ENGLISH part-time at the local state
university when I lived in Sebastopol. The college was new,
innovative, and on the cutting edge intellectually. They had
debated about where to build it—whether it should be up on
Sonoma Mountain or west, in the redwoods by the Russian
River, but they finally built it halfway between, on a low lying swampy plain. I think this was a mistake. Indeed, for a
while, low enrollment kept everyone demoralized and afraid
for their jobs.

But then, little by little, the marshy fields which surrounded the college began to fill up with tract houses. The
chairman of the English Department moved into a small one,
and within a few years, a newer, larger one. He was a Dickens
freak. Once a week, several of us who were also anglophiles
would gather at his tract house in a cul-de-sac built over the

swamp near the college and read aloud from one Dickens book after another.

I came to dread the meetings of the Dickens Circle. In the world of Dickens, each eccentric character occupied a real place in a fixed world filled with smoke and stone, already old and attached to history. The contrast between this and the desolate anonymous tract house with its fresh sheet rock and the glare of the California sun in its plate glass window made me feel hopeless.

Our chairman sat in his Lazy Boy lounger sucking on his pipe. One day in early September, out on the cedar shavings in the front of his house and in front of his wife and four teenage children, our chairman poured gasoline over himself and lit a match.

One Wonderful Thing

ONE WONDERFUL THING JOHN HATFIELD did to the house in Sebastopol was to open the western wall of the small bedroom with a set of French doors leading out to a wooden deck. The deck was built around the existing trees, and overhung with lilac. This was a beautiful private place to sit in the sun. Unfortunately, the winter storms came from the west, and the deck soon began to warp. The French doors became swollen and difficult to open.

There was a covered porch on the north side of the house, and the real front door to the house opened onto it. However, people rarely used this door, as you had to go down the driveway and up the garden path to get to the porch steps. There was a door from the kitchen leading out to this porch, also, and a giant hydrangea, like a paddle wheel, in front of it.

The most logical entrance to the house was through the back door, but after my new husband and I bought this house

69

we sealed off this door so that we could make the back porch into a nursery. I had gotten pregnant on our wedding night. The baby room turned out to be one of the nicest rooms in the house. It faced south and east. Outside was the orchard. I put gauzy white curtains on the windows and fabric with little birds on it over the door which was sealed, but still there. It was apple blossom time when our baby first sat up in her crib. She sat and looked out her window as the whole world came into blossom.

It was about a year later, after her sister was born, that we decided quite precipitously to move to New York. We were not going to need a car where we were going, and both of our old Volkswagens died within a few days of hearing the news. I think they had a suicide pact.

We had, of course, never done any of the improvements on the house which we had dreamed of doing, and I think the house must have resented this, or perhaps it was angry at being abandoned, because first the French doors stopped opening altogether and then the kitchen door, which had never before given us any trouble, closed and refused to open. For the last few days we were there we had to go all through the house to the living room to get out. This, of course, made it difficult to show the house to prospective buyers. Indeed, we had been living in New York a full year before the house sold.

Still, the last day we were there, after the movers had come and stripped the house bare of every personal object which belonged to us, when the house was just itself again, we all walked from room to room, saying goodbye to each corner. I was able to express my anger at the house's behavior then, and to thank it for everything it had done for me. And so I severed myself from that place forever.

II. The Great Room of the House Resembled an Ark

All My Life

ALL MY LIFE I HAD PROMISED myself that I would live in New York at least one year. I wanted to know what it was like to live in the snow. As a child I was taken to walk around in the snow up on Mt. Baldy two or three times, but this did little to initiate me into its mystery. The ride there was long and I never knew what shoes to wear. I was afraid to walk in it. I didn't know if I would slip. Still, what I was less prepared for than the snow in New York were the electrical storms, the explosive warm rains that characterize the summer.

After we left Sebastopol, we went first to visit my husband's family in Pleasantville, a small town about forty minutes north of Manhattan. We were on our way to Jerusalem, where my husband was going to study before he began school in Manhattan in the fall. I remember that it was June, because our new baby had been born the first of

May, and we had to prop up her head so they could take her passport picture. She was six weeks old, the age a kitten has to be before it can leave its mother.

We thought of ourselves as supremely fertile. We had been married during the most powerful storm of the year, when the Russian River had overflowed its banks. Trees has bowed down and seeds were carried everywhere. In the midst of this, our baby had taken hold, and her little sister had followed only twenty months after.

When we left Sebastopol, we disburdened ourselves of all but the most essential of our earthly possessions. I was full of hope, and I was also full of milk. The baby was still so new that my breasts had not yet regulated themselves, and milk was always leaking from me. I was already wet and sticky, and it was uncomfortably hot when we got to Pleasantville, where my husband's family gathered us into their home.

The air was dense, more dense than it ever was in California. My clothes were sticking to me. My husband motioned for me to look up at the rafters in the ceiling. Then I saw what he had described to me many times before. The great room of the house resembled an ark.

The room was suddenly dark, and then there was thunder. Lightning illuminated our faces a brief moment. My husband and I looked at each other. Our babies were on our laps. We were setting out on a great adventure.

Then the rain came pouring down on the house. It beat on the roof and pounded on the flagstone terrace, and the waters ran hissing into the garden.

One Day, Shortly After

ONE DAY, SHORTLY AFTER WE had come back from Jerusalem to
New York for the second time, after we had been living there
a year, we decided to take the girls to the Bronx Zoo. They
were three and four now. I took them every day to the
playground in Riverside Park where they played with children
of all different colors who were speaking all different
languages. The first time we went my older girl came up to
tell me that there were *Aravim* in the sandbox. When she
heard the children speaking Spanish, a language she didn't
know, she assumed they were Arabs.

I had taken the girls to the little zoo in Jerusalem where
we learned the word for swans—*barburim*, and we had all
gone to the Safari where lions ran free outside the town of
Ramat Gan near Tel Aviv, but none of us had ever been to
the Bronx Zoo. Because we had no car, we took the subway,
and we huddled together as we rode, staring silently at the

people sitting opposite us who started blankly back. Some of the people on the train were African, some Asian, some European.

Suddenly the train came above ground and a pale blue light illuminated the faces in the car. Outside were the burned-out desolate deserted buildings of the South Bronx. The train careened over the tracks. There was no particular reason why any of us in that car should have been there. We or our parents or our parents' parents had come here only to escape being some place else. None of us really belonged here, I thought, as I looked at my reflection in the faces of my fellow passengers. Then I was overcome by a longing for the pink stone of Jerusalem.

I Used to Take

I USED TO TAKE THE GIRLS UP on the hill across the street from our apartment in Jerusalem at sunset. This was the border between our neighborhood and a Bedouin village. Little boys herded their goats past us. The goats bleated and shook their bells. A few wildflowers grew in the stony ground. We climbed the big rocks and looked west with the setting sun, and we watched as the Old City turned to gold.

There is a city ordinance in Jerusalem that requires all buildings to be built out of Jerusalem stone, a limestone quarried just outside the city. It is a color between pink and yellow. The thick stone walls of our building helped to keep our apartment cool in hot weather. Birds nested in the window ledges. I listened to their liquid warbling as I lay in my daughters' darkened room, cradling them as they resisted sleep.

Because of the stone, one neighborhood was not so very different from the next. I was not so conscious here, as I was in New York, of class differences. Everyone was in the same situation. It was a great leveler.

In Jerusalem there is another ordinance, I believe, which forbids burial in wooden boxes. This is perhaps because wood is so precious here, or perhaps because the wood would impede one's return into the holy land. At one time, however, all the stony mountains of Jerusalem were covered with forests of oak, cedar and myrtle. These were, apparently, all cut down by the Romans, intent on their building projects.

When the Romans first laid siege to the city, the stone kept them out. But then they sent flaming arrows. The Jerusalem stone began to hiss, and then to explode. The huge Herodian stones flew from the Temple. I saw some of these where they landed on an archeological tour one morning.

And now I walked down the hill along the curving edge of the stone apartment complexes. Some butterflies must have just hatched out, because thousands were being lifted in the wind in front of me, across my path. It was strange to think that they were only going to live a few weeks. I passed the stone community center where my daughters had taken ballet lessons with its red Calder cow in front and I made my way to the bus stop. I had just gotten a letter from New York saying that they had found an apartment for us. Now we would not stay in Jerusalem another year. We had been toying with that idea. We had left it up to the housing situation to determine our fate. I was feeling very confused and anxious about where home was. I was on my way downtown to meet my husband and give him the news.

I leaned against a wall and waited for the bus. Then a gust of warm wind scattered the dust at my feet and lifted the dry chalky odor out of the Jerusalem stone. It permeated the air. How particular, how familiar it was. I already missed it. It smelled like bones.

Two Swans Were on the Lake

TWO SWANS WERE ON THE LAKE last evening when I walked the dog. This spring has been particularly beautiful. The flowering cherries have already peaked and now their blossoms blow across the lawn like pink snow. The burnt rose dogwood and the vermilion azalea are all in bloom.

My niece visited me about two months ago. She's from the West, and has never lived where there are deciduous trees. As we drove along she looked up at Bear Mountain and said that it looked like Arizona. All the trees were still leafless sticks; the mountain was a monotonous brown.

By the next week, however, I could see that the sap was running. The twiggy branches began to be tinged with color, pink, purple, and red, like blood.

"So, they're alive," I thought. When I had first visited in the East and saw all the deciduous trees in leaf it meant nothing to me. It was fall. Everyone said, "Look at the beautiful fall foliage," but it only annoyed me. It reminded me of the mural on the wall in my accountant's office. I missed my bare California hills, covered with golden grass, with oak trees only in the gullies where the creeks run in the winter.

But now I realize what the problem was. The fall foliage only derives its meaning from its relationship to the full luxuriance of summer. And so, also, the spring touches me now because I, too, am beginning to flower after the bare sticks of winter.

The evenings are long now, and warm, and it is a good time to walk the dog. We passed a house which I am particularly fond of because of its pagoda roofs. It is partially obscured now by some red maples which are suddenly in leaf.

We turned the corner and I noticed how even the plain and ugly houses in the neighborhood have been softened and transformed by the spring, by their dogwood, lilacs and maples.

We came upon a very poor house. It is a small Cape Cod with nothing to recommend it. When people put up their Christmas decorations in the winter a line of plastic soldiers in red uniforms lined each side of the path that leads from the road to its door. These did not light up and looked quite sad.

But now two trees which I never noticed before have come into leaf on each side of the path. Their leaves join and form one full round shape in front of the house. These are red maples. They are dark crimson underneath and shine blood red above.

I see into the house through the branches of the trees. It is getting to be night and the people have lighted their lights. There is life inside the house.

The Air Is Like Wine

THE AIR IS LIKE WINE TODAY. The wind rushes in the trees. Last night there was a tremendous storm with lightning and thunder and torrents of rain. We were awakened in the middle of the night by the phone.

Another emergency. The place where my husband works seems to be having a serious financial crisis. It may be on the verge of collapse. We had already decided to leave after one more year, but now we wonder if we shouldn't try to leave sooner. My husband says that it may to too late in the season to find another position, however. What will we do if it turns out that they are unable to pay him for the time he remains?

But how can I worry about this when the day is so perfect, so pure, so fresh. The trees have grown full overnight, and the birds are chittering.

The dog couldn't wait to get outside this morning. There was a cool edge of excitement in the air. A pair of geese with their goslings were in the shallow water at the edge of the lake. The lake was a deep blue. There were waves on the lake. It is hard to believe that anything bad could happen on a day like this.

When I went away to college I lived, at first, in a dorm. My room was on the eighth floor, facing west, and I had a view of the San Francisco Bay. My whole life was ahead of me, like they say, and I didn't know what was going to happen.

I looked out at the Bay. Sometimes it was green, sometimes it was blue, sometimes it was grey. It looked different at different times of the day. It looked different from day to day. Each time I looked at it, it had changed.

When I Imagined

WHEN I IMAGINED MY HUSBAND giving notice, which he has, I thought of the time, a little over a year which extends ahead of us to the end when we will leave, as a fallow period. The term "lame duck" was the caption for the picture. However, it has not turned out that way at all. In fact, this has turned out to be an oddly delicious time. If things go wrong here now it is no longer something which is going to affect me for the rest of my life.

In Sebastopol, I used to walk in Swain Woods every day. It was an oak forest not far from my house. But one day, the bulldozers came and began to level the trees, and Swain Woods began to turn into Swain Estates. After that, I restricted my wanderings to the orchards, knowing it was just a matter of time before they went. They may be gone now, for all I know, but that possibility can no longer disturb me.

I'm sure as the year wears on I will grow more and more anxious about where we are going, but from this distance all I can see is the infinity of possibility. And because I know the end is coming, I think I love this house where we are now more purely than I ever did before. I no longer have the need to impose my will on the house, to "improve" it, but rather, I see my role now only as caretaker. I am taking care of the house, keeping it in order and opening its windows so that it can breath the spring air. I am not worrying that the house is going to feel too small when the girls are teenagers. They do not know it yet, but they won't be here when they are.

This is a perfect childhood house. There is something ineffably cozy about it. Trees look into all the windows. Morning light comes into all the bedrooms. Behind the house is a large screened room which the people in these parts refer to as a gazebo, but it's more like a pavilion. It's barn red, and has beds built into the wall. The children like to paint out there, and we have their birthday parties there. I make them a chocolate cake with white icing, like my mother always made for my birthdays.

I've put some swings in the ash tree which is just outside the gazebo. There they can swing almost up into the lilacs, and then there is, of course, all the rolling lawn, and the neighborhood children coming and going on their bikes, the lake, and the creek across the road full of crayfish and frogs.

I've made a nook in the living room, a futon couch in the corner of the wall with a bookcase enclosing it at the other end where the girls have their books, their art supplies and a little t.v. They love to curl up there on the giant pillows with the dog. There they do their homework, and draw and dream. I bring them snacks there on trays, and sometimes even their dinner when their Daddy's working late.

Their rooms are on either side of ours. They can call us from their beds, and we'll come and tuck them in again.

The dogwood in my daughters' bedroom windows is in flower now. But although I had it trimmed and fertilized last fall, part of it still looks dead. Perhaps this year or next year will be the last season for this tree, but I won't be here to see the house once it's bereft. It's not that I am no longer concerned with or involved with this tree now that I am leaving, but the nature of my concern has changed. If the tree needs to die, then I am here, no longer to resent or resist this condition, but simply to observe it.

My Husband Lived

MY HUSBAND LIVED IN AN APARTMENT in Brooklyn until he was seven. He was the first grandchild in the family on both sides, and was generally adored. There was a long hallway where he used to play, and, of course, the street. But then his parents built their dream house up in the country, near Pleasantville. They were part of a group which bought land communally and had houses built by Frank Lloyd Wright and his students. It was Wright's experiment, to try to build houses for ordinary people, and he gave the place its name—Usonia. All the Usonians were struggling young professionals then, but eventually they all became prosperous, and each family obtained ownership of its own parcel of land.

Still, there remained a strong community feeling. Children would go into whatever house they were near for lunch when they were out playing. They had, and still have, communal parties on holidays. The Usonians are getting old now, and many have died, but no one has ever moved out, and some of the second generation have moved back, including my husband's sister and her family, who have a house just over the hill from my mother-in-law, who, like many of her friends, is now widowed. My husband's sister was only four when the family moved to Usonia, and hardly has a memory of anywhere else.

My husband's little brother was born the year they moved, and never really had any other home. Even though he lives in Massachusetts now, he comes most weekends with his family to stay with his mother and sit in his father's chair.

I remember when my father-in-law died, how terrified everyone was in the immediate as well as the larger family that my mother-in-law would lose her house. That house is a sacred family institution. My mother-in-law is the eldest of four sisters, and although all of them have grown wealthy and acquired beautiful houses of their own, my in-laws were the first to do so, and their house was somehow deified.

My children sense this, also, and share in the workship of the house. However, although we are only forty minutes away, we hardly ever go there. My husband's work schedule is too hectic, and the children have school, and after school, lessons. We used to try to go there on Sundays when we lived in Manhattan, especially in the summer. I was desperate to get the girls into some fresh air. Usonia is set in the woods. The house has rolling lawns and formal gardens. There's a swimming pool and swings, terraces, a grand piano, and a play room. It was difficult to get there, however, as we had no car, and it was depressing and somewhat scary to take the train from the 125th Street station.

When my husband was a child, he shared a room with his little brother. There were three bedrooms, all in a line. Their sister had her own room between the boys' room and their parents. The boys had bunk beds. My husband adored his baby brother. He loved to teach him things. But then their

87

parents noticed that the baby was destroying his brother's homework.

So they hired the famous Japanese architect, Kahn Demoto, to transform the garage, which sat beneath the main house, into a room for my husband. The room had a long built-in desk looking out at the woods, where his parents imagined him studying away. It was large and cheerful, with accents of primary colors, and he could try all sorts of athletic feats on the floor. He had his own radio and his own t.v., and there he developed his love of the media, sports, and things Japanese.

No one ever visited him down there. It would have been an invasion. However, he often invited his baby brother down to join him in his sports fantasies. His little brother grew bigger and more athletic than he was as the years wore on, so these games became less pleasant.

There were several months during the renovation of the kitchen when the family used my husband's room as a makeshift kitchen. This was still his room, he was still sleeping there, but the family also ate all their meals there.

There was a little bathroom down there which he shared with the West Indian maid, who also had a room down there. Her room was just behind the wall that his bed was pushed up against, where he lay reading mildly pornographic magazines, adjacent to the laundry, and she walked through his room on her way upstairs to clean the house.

My husband's parents wanted to protect him from his baby brother, and from the screams of his sister, who had to have several operations on her leg, and later, from the screaming fights his sister had with his mother about what she was wearing to school each day. My husband's father was often ill, and often being taken to the hospital, but alone down in his basement room, my husband was protected from all this. And that was how he came to occupy the position of outsider in the family.

My Husband's Father

MY HUSBAND'S FATHER WAS VERY ill for many years before he died, and dependent upon his wife to care for him. I remember, right before our second daughter was born, my mother-in-law came out to California to help me prepare, and she was called home after just a few days. Her husband was afraid to be without her.

He required all her attention. He must have known he was going to die. Because she loved him best, she stopped paying attention to the other great love of her life—her house—and it began to suffer from neglect.

It bothered the house that even after my husband's father was gone it still didn't get the attention it craved from its woman, for she was cast into a state of deep and single-minded mourning, so I'm afraid it resorted to some pretty desperate measures to get her attention.

First, its roof went. Apparently it had been rotting for

quite a while, and no one had ever noticed, though the smell of mildew pervaded the house and was especially strong in the den, where we stayed for a few days on our way to Israel.

The den was not part of the original house, and my husband had told me many times how this addition had destroyed, for him, the integrity of the original design, which had been ark-like and perfect. It was built along the north wall of the living room, and for this reason alone it was necessarily dark and damp. But they put their hide-a-bed couch there and their largest t.v. and my husband's father's black leather chair with its hassock.

The original roof had been cedar shingles, but when this had started to need repairs my husband's father had hired his secretary's husband, who was then out of work, to put a new roof on. It was an act of kindness. The man was not really a roofer, and agreed to do the work for much less than a real roofer would ask.

My husband's father wanted to get rid of the cedar shingles, because he was deathly afraid of fire, so he had his secretary's husband put asbestos shingles on, instead. However, the man didn't ventilate the roof properly, and after that, the house began to suffocate.

Another problem had to do with the trees and vines which grew up against the north side of the house. When the house was first built, my husband's father went off into the woods and brought back a wild vine which he planted against the house. Now my husband's father was gone, and the vine was undermining the house.

The vine had to go. Men in work clothes came and wrenched the thing out of my mother-in-law's heart. "Look, you can see the stars now," I said, trying to comfort her, but she was white and stricken.

It was clear to me that this was a war the house was waging against the memory of my husband's father, or maybe my husband's father was still an active adversary, though weakened by death. Who knows about these things. At any rate, this was only the first battle. Heat pipes broke in the floor, so that the living room had to be excavated, the kitchen floor buckled, and my mother-in-law's toilet stopped flushing.

But then something wonderful happened. My husband's brother, who was divorced and unhappy, became engaged, and asked his mother to make a great wedding for him in the house. And so my mother-in-law turned her gaze to the future, when the new family her son was about to make would come to occupy her house. Her new focus was so intense, that the house succumbed and began to cooperate.

The wedding was beautiful. The house could not have been more gracious, except for the fact that it couldn't resist tripping my mother-in-law on one of its steps and spraining her ankle. However, this did not keep her from dancing.

I think some equilibrium has been reached now. My husband's brother's family comes to occupy the house periodically, but then they go. I've heard people speculate about my mother-in-law, why she wishes to continue alone in that huge house with all its responsibilities, but I know she will never leave it, and I don't think the house would let her, even if she wanted to.

I've seen the light coming into my mother-in-law's kitchen in the morning, and I've seen her gaze go up over the cabinets, all carefully waxed, to the clerestory windows, and then travel lovingly over the angles of intersection between ceiling and wall.

It Might Be Surprising

IT MIGHT BE SURPRISING TO some people to hear me express what might be taken as pagan sentiments, since my husband is a rabbi. However, it says in the book of *Leviticus* that a house can have leprosy, and it devotes several lines to explaining how to get the leprosy out of the house, which mainly entails having a priest come to look at it three times and then, if the leprosy is still there, leveling the house. So perhaps I am examining all these houses to see if they have leprosy.

There is a lot written in the book of *Exodus*, also, specifying the architectural details of the Tabernacle, and at the heart of Judaism is the Temple and the Temple Cult. "Temple" is a Greek word; in Hebrew, it was called a house.

I may be equally influenced, however, by that other great religion, Americanism, in which words like "dreamhouse" and "homeowner" are central to the liturgy. I grew up during the post-war housing boom, and my father made his living by virtue of the growth of the construction industry.

Now, however, the housing market is "soft." The "for sale" signs that were up in my neighborhood last summer are still up. I'm glad that we didn't strain ourselves to buy our house. It wasn't necessary. The landlord's not going to sell the house out from under us, and now we are leaving.

Part of the reason we are leaving has to do with the housing market being "soft." The area is stagnating. My husband would like to work in a place that is growing.

Last night we were visited by some friends from my husband's Seminary days, one a rabbi in Nebraska, and the other in Montreal. Naturally, I asked them if they would describe their houses to me. In many congregations there is a house provided for the rabbi within walking distance of the synagogue, and both these friends live in such houses.

"It's a split-level," both friends said, and this didn't surprise me, since the split-level or bi-level is quite common and the cheapest house to build. "It's in fairly good condition," my friend's wife from Montreal said. Rabbis' houses are always low-maintenance. "I like it because there's only a few steps up to the kids' rooms and a few steps down to ours, and that's good for my back."

My husband was looking at me. I could tell he was worried I was going to say something, because he knows of my irrational aversion to split-level houses. I feel schizophrenic when I am in a split-level house. I never know exactly where I am, up or down. There's no center.

"The only thing is," my Montreal friend went on, "even though there is plenty of room, the slightest noise travels all over the house. You can hear everything—except from the basement. The kids have this big playroom down there."

I know that in many split level houses the basement is used as a playroom. I once took my children to play with some chldren who lived in one. We entered the playroom through the garage. There packages of toilet paper were piled to the ceiling. There must have been a sale.

Another time my husband and I went to the bi-level house of some congregants. There was no level that the front door led to. I looked down, then I held on to the iron rail as we climbed the short flight of steps, so that we were now looking into the kitchen. Instead of leading us right, into the living room, they led us down a narrow hall to their bedroom. It was heavy with dark furniture. I could see wedding pictures hanging on the grey walls through the dim light. Then they showed us their son's room. It was painted black. We were there because my husband is a rabbi and they needed him to look at their house.

One of the Things

ONE OF THE THINGS WHICH appealed to me about this place when my husband first took a job here was that the synagogue was not built to be a synagogue, it was, originally, a house.

It was a very large house, of course, with many windows and a lot of mahogany woodwork. They transformed the double garage into a small two-bedroom apartment for the rabbi and his family, and we still stay there on the sabbath and holidays, when we don't drive, since the house we are renting is three miles away. In the bedroom my husband and I share there is a large bank of windows looking out on the woods. This was taken out of the upstairs sanctuary wall where they have put the ark, and behind this hollow wall some birds have built a nest now, and I like to watch them flying back and forth just outside the window during services.

When we agreed to come here, the congregation promised to build a house for us in the meadow behind the synagogue.

Harriet Balaran, an architect who is one of the congregants, and who has become one of my closest friends, drew up the plans for it.

She talked to me about what I wanted and designed it that way, within the cost limitation. For example, I wanted the light to come from at least two directions, and so she drew windows on two sides of each room. The windows were all different shapes and sizes. Another striking feature of the house is in the roof line, which is basically barn-shaped. There is a broken pediment. This was a form popular in the Renaissance, Harriet explained to me, based on the idea that shapes that are broken will nonetheless have reference to wholeness, will evoke wholeness more thoroughly than a continuous form because our imaginations will constantly be filling in the lines.

She gave me a copy of the plans, and I spent many hours inhabiting that house, climbing the stairs and entering each room. There was a large window over the landing in the stairs, and this was a particularly sunny spot where I would always pause.

However, the house was never built. They had not yet gotten the building permit when it was time for us to move, so we rented the lake house, thinking it would only be temporary. But once we had settled in, we realized that we didn't want them to build Harriet's house. The location was too isolated, and we were now enjoying being in a neighborhood full of children. Or perhaps the idea of moving again was simply too tiring. But I had other reservations about the house, also, which I couldn't quite dismiss. Every time I climbed the hill and stood on the site where the house was to be built, and pretended I was in one room or another, I was always vexed by the low roar of the Thruway which couldn't be seen but which ran just over the rise. It never stopped. There was never silence.

The other day Harriet came to visit. She knows I am

leaving and is quite upset. She told me she had had a dream about me. She had dreamed that she was coming to visit me and she was driving around my neighborhood looking for my house. She was worried, because she didn't know where I lived. the houses were quite nondescript. Could I be living in a nondescript house? Then she saw my house, and it was all built out of amber colored wood. It was small and cozy looking. There was a broken pediment in the roof line, and I was waving at her from one of the little windows.

Harriet's Mother Is Very Ill

HARRIET'S MOTHER IS VERY ILL. She has cancer, which was discovered shortly after Harriet's father died, suddenly, of a heart attack, about a year ago. She thought at first that she got it because as soon as her husband died she decided to sell the family house in Far Rockaway and move to Manhattan. She felt it was a betrayal of her dead husband.

She had wanted to sell the family home for the past fifteen years, since her husband retired and began to spend all of his time in the house, in his den. He was extremely untidy, and it was impossible to keep the house up. However, he wouldn't even consider moving.

Harriet's mother just lost interest in the house. Now that her husband was home, she spent most of her time out, working for various worthy causes. However, the house had begun its life as a dreamhouse. Harriet remembers, as I remember, as my husband remembers, driving to the site where the family dreamhouse was being constructed and walking around inside its skeleton.

When Harriet was about twelve, her mother hired a decorator to redo the house. Her name was Nancy Chase. She was a large woman with a clear voice who always dressed in black.

She did the den all in black with Eames chairs. The living room acquired a lot of horizontal woodwork. Nancy Chase and Harriet's mother fought a lot, but nonetheless Nancy became deified in Harriet's family. Perhaps this was why Harriet became an architect—so that her mother would admire her as she had admired Nancy Chase. However, no one could ever live up to Nancy Chase. She was a goddess of design.

Harriet's husband, who is a doctor, advised her mother not to sell her Far Rockaway house and move to the city. He thought she would become too sick too soon for this to be practical. However, this has not proved to be the case.

The apartment she found is in midtown Manhattan in the building where her sister and several of her friends live. She has hired a decorator who has chosen beautiful silk fabric to reupholster the furniture in. Harriet had hoped she would choose fabrics more conducive to having her grandchildren visit. She had imagined her mother wanting to spend all the time she could with her grandchildren now that she was ill. Harriet's children are one and four. But this style of decorating is one Nancy Chase would have approved of.

"This is what makes your mother happy," I remind Harriet. Then I ask her how her visit to her mother was on Monday. Naturally, I am curious about what her new apartment is like.

"It was very odd," Harriet said. "Her furniture is still being upholstered so that the apartment is absolutely bare. It was odd to see my mother living with a card table and a folding chair. It was like seeing her naked."

"Just as her head is naked under her wig now," I said.

"Mothers should have their furniture around them," Harriet said. "I felt bad for her, but she didn't seem unhappy and the apartment was extremely sunny. From her window she has a beautiful view of all these ragged rooflines with water towers, dark red and grey.

"And she has a view of all these terraces and roof gardens, which are all starting to bloom now. But what is really nice is tht she can see into a school yard where children are playing. She can watch the children play, but she can't hear their voices."

My Father's First Office

MY FATHER'S FIRST OFFICE WAS at the house on Genesee, in a little room off the garage. I don't remember him actually working there, but later, when he had an office elsewhere, how the room was dark and dusty and full of grey things.

Eventually, my father bought his own building, and then several buildings, but now, forty-five years later, my father feels he is getting too old to continue, so he has sold the business to someone else.

I don't think either of my parents anticipated how devastating this would be for them. But now, according to my mother, my father is walking around in shock, like a zombie. My mother is in acute distress. They are not going to have as much money as they are used to having. They are convinced that they have made a mistake.

Unfortunately, at the same time, my husband and I are also suffering economically. We did not anticipate what our taxes would be, and so we have gone badly into debt. I had half hoped my parents would be able to help us out, but I can't ask them now, now that they are so upset about their own finances. And I know they are planning to use what capital they think they can spare to fix up the family house. It is getting old now, and they want it to be comfortable and trouble-free for their old age, which, though they are both in good health and look extremely youthful, is just around the corner.

I wonder if my husband and I will ever have a house to fix up so our old age is comfortable. This doesn't seem likely; we seem to have lost our chance a long time ago. I have a close friend, Paula Spector, who is exactly my age, but she and her husband have been married twenty years to our ten. When she was first married they bought a little piece of property which they were able to sell for a large profit and invest in a larger piece of property which they were able to sell last year when they built their big beautiful dreamhouse. However, my husband and I have never managed to get a foothold on the ladder of property ownership, and I don't see how we ever will, now.

This hasn't bothered me, however, perhaps because I always knew my parents were there behind us if we ever got in trouble. But now my husband and I will just have to tighten our belts. Still, I don't want my children to have to give anything up.

Yesterday evening, when the girls were watching t.v. in the nook in the corner of the living room, I took the dog out for his walk. Night was just falling. The trees were suddenly dark shapes. Lights began to glow in the houses, and I could see inside through the windows half open. Then I came upon my own house. Someone had left the back porchlight on by mistake, and it was illuminating the back yard unnaturally. Lights blazed in every window. All the shades were wide open, exposing everything inside. I ran up the steps. My children were huddled in the corner of the living room. I let go of the dog and yanked at the cords to lower the blinds by their heads. And so I fled from room to room, pulling down shades and turning off lights.

A Tree Has Died

A TREE HAS DIED IN MY FRONT yard. I am afraid that this house is already becoming vindictive. It was a pretty little flowering cherry and must have died when the gardener removed the hedge that stood in front of it that was all covered with poison ivy. He sprayed the ground with herbicide and the little tree died.

I am very sad about the little tree and I feel guilty. It was I who asked the gardener to remove the hedge. I feel like I have failed utterly, that it is because of people like me that the earth is dying.

Virginia came with me to walk the dog today and she understands my despair and my guilt. She is a Master Gardener. Yesterday she showed me the virburnum flowering in her yard which she planted five years ago. Its white flowers stand straight up from the branches and, from a distance, there appears to have been a late snowfall. How pleasant that must be to see something which was quite small when you planted it grow large and healthy. To plant something small you must believe in the future.

"Can you keep a secret?" I asked Virginia. "We are leaving next year." We were passing a white house with two black benches in front. These benches are the same as the green bench to the side of my front door. There used to be two green benches, but one rotted out and fell backwards off the porch into the rhododendron bush, much to the surprise of the neighbor child who was sitting in it.

Another neighbor once suggested to me that I knock on the door of the white house with the black benches and ask the people where they got their benches so I could replace mine. But I never did, and I never saw any people going or coming from that house until today—a woman with a withered arm.

My Aunt Lil

MY AUNT LIL WAS A HOUSEWIFE, and I suppose she still is, although she has been widowed for many years now and no longer lives in the house she was once married to, but has moved with all the beautiful Stickley furniture that once inhabited that house to a small apartment near Century City. However, that house that she belonged to, where she lived with my Uncle Jack and their Airedale, Ruff, who was already a ghost, a photograph, a porcelain figurine, by the time I awoke conscious in the midst of my family, was on Warner Avenue, close to U.C.L.A.

My Aunt Lil and my Uncle Jack never had any children, though they wanted them dearly, and they were like grandparents to me and my sister. Uncle Jack was round and bald and jolly, and Aunt Lil was silver haired and sweet. Our father was her baby brother, she had practically raised him, and my sister and I occasionally spent the night at their house. My uncle had a candy factory, and I saw him cooking candy with a candy thermometer in a big pot on the stove. We played with the big silver hourglass that sat on a table in the living room and looked at the four drinking glasses on each of which a neighbor across the road had painted a likeness of Aunt Lil and Uncle Jack's house. They had a four poster bed with a green satin comforter and a pretty little sewing table with a bright red pincushion and a silver thimble and silver scissors for cutting grapes. Unlike us, they had a basement, but my sister and I were afraid to go down there. We liked to climb to the hot unfinished room over the garage where the rug my aunt was hooking was waiting to be worked on. This, however, was never finished. But what we loved most was to play croquet on the grass between my aunt's rose bushes when we went there for holidays.

It was at Aunt Lil's house that we and all our aunts and uncles and cousins had all of our holiday dinners. The table was set before we arrived. Our aunt was in her apron, basting the turkey. We would stand in the kitchen with its rooster wallpaper while our uncle poured us our root beers. From here we went into the den to build with the wooden blocks, which, I realize only now, were scraps from a construction site collected for kindling. On the Fourth of July, when there no longer was enough light to see the croquet ball and we began tripping on the wickets, my uncle would light firecrackers on the cement beneath the back porch. My favorite was the burning house, because I thought this one was safe.

After dinner we sat on the floor in the living room, playing cards with the cousins we never saw at other times, and cracking nuts, while the grown-ups sat in the beautiful chairs my aunt, a talented seamstress, had made slipcovers for, and our Uncle Lou, whom no one ever spoke to, dozed on the couch.

These holidays when I sat at the dark wood table, those

nights when I slept on the couch in the den or days when I climbed the hill at the end of the garden and lay down in the tall grass by the orange trees which still exist, as every action loosed in the world continues forever, though my uncle died suddenly in his sleep and my aunt sold the house for a loss and burned all the photographs. Now when I take my children to visit her in her apartment they turn over the silver hourglass and watch the sand sift through, and then I show them the four glasses, still unbroken, where the house with its bay window and cedar shingles still encloses me and my sister and my parents and aunts and uncles and cousins.

I Needed a Gift

I NEEDED A GIFT, SO I WENT to the bookstore in town today. It's a tiny bookstore, but I never fail to find everything I want there, and if I do, Gerry, the owner, orders it for me. She is a very pleasant person, and over the past few years we have become friends.

Gerry is a widow. Her husband died suddenly of a heart attack a few years ago when she was only thirty-nine. This happened just before she opened her store, and the store has been a husband to her, jealous of her attention, ever since. So now she is selling the store and moving to California. Her daughter graduated from high school this year. In the spring, they went to California together to look at colleges and real estate, and as soon as the business sells, they will be leaving.

"All my life," Gerry confided in me one day, "I have lived in houses that were a good investment. My husband and I moved many times, and each time we had to buy a house that would be easy to sell, that had a certain amount of space, a certain number of bathrooms, that was a standard design. But this is where I want to live," she said, opening a book which she kept on the counter. Inside was a tiny cottage amongst the redwoods in California.

"When we were in California," Gerry said to me, "I went around with a real estate woman in Mendocino, and she told me that this place wasn't for everyone, but at the end of the day, after we had been together looking at houses, she told me that she could see that I did belong there."

That seemed true to me. I know the Mendocino coast and can very easily picture Gerry there. But it is odd to think that a person raised on a farm in Wisconsin who spent her adult life in the Hudson Valley actually belongs in a cottage in Mendocino with hollyhocks in front looming through the fog.

One day when I was in her store browsing in the architecture section she came and told me that her house had sold. Everything was going on schedule. She even had some people interested in buying the store. When she had first told me that she was selling the store I had been horrified. I couldn't imagine anyone else running it. But now that I am leaving too, this no longer matters to me. "I am going to go through all my things very carefully now," she said. "I'm only going to take with me what I absolutely need, just the things I really care about, not all those things that have been weighing me down all these years."

"The house closed weeks ago," she told me when I arrived in the store today. "My daughter and I are renting an apartment in Washingtonville now. I put everything in storage. I put it in Beckwith's. I was going to use one of those self-store places, but they just look so vulnerable. I wanted to be safe, so I put everything in Beckwith's where there was a guard watching over everything, and last week there was a fire. Beckwith's burned to the ground. I lost everything."

"Oh, Gerry!" I said.

"I spent months going through everything," Gerry said. "This was only the stuff I really wanted to keep."

"It must have been insured," I said.

"But how can I ever replace the jar of my daughter's baby teeth? The hunk of her hair from when she had long hair? Her baby book? My photo album? The needlepoint I did, her baby pillow I embroidered, all the letters my husband and I wrote to each other, the poems we sent each other? I went through everything," she said, "so slowly and carefully, and I examined each object and I read every letter. I said to myself, this is foolish, to go through all of this, all the objects which tie me to my past, so slowly. I didn't know I was saying good-bye to them forever. Sure, I can buy another copy of the *Odyssey*, but it won't have my notes in it. I had kept the wall calendars I had used for years. And in these I could see when we went to the dentist and when Aunt Mary visited. I can never get these back."

"I'm just angry," Gerry said. "I'm angrier than when my husband died. That I could almost understand. I don't know who I'm angry at—certainly not Beckwith's. Can you imagine how they must feel? To be responsible for so many people losing what's precious to them? Why couldn't it have happened four weeks ago, before I put my stuff there? This I can't understand. My daughter says we will start a new history when we go to California, and I know this will be true for her. She is just beginning life. I am so angry and I don't know who to be angry at."

"But don't you have some of your own things in the apartment you're renting?" I asked.

"All we have is a couch, two chairs, a table and two lamps, and my daughter's bedroom set in the bedroom. The apartment is tiny. It's only three rooms. There's only one bathroom. We're sharing a bathroom. But it's wonderful! It's so small that we have to be close. If one of us is on the couch and the other one is at the table, we are still together. We haven't been this close since she was a little girl peeking out from behind my skirts. And in the middle of this, all the remnants of her babyhood burn up in the fire! She's leaving for college at the end of the summer. I never expected to have this time with her, and it may never happen again. It's been a gift."

We Spent the Fourth of July

WE SPENT THE FOURTH OF JULY at my husband's mother's house. It was a hot day, and close. The children bobbed in and out of the pool. The thunderstorms, which had been predicted, never materialized, but a wind rushed in the trees.

"I love those trees," my husband's mother said. "Can you imagine how old they must be? They were that tall when we moved here, forty years ago." She turned in her lounge chair to look at me. It is hard to believe she is seventy, her face is so lovely. I looked up at the screened porches which overhang the terrace. At one time, there was one porch that ran the length of all three bedrooms. On hot summer nights the family would drag their mattresses and their t.v. out there, and there they would sleep, all of them together.

But the middle bedroom, my husband's sister's bedroom, was very small, and when she became a teenager they extended her room so that it included her portion of the

113

screened porch, leaving two small screened porches, cut off from each other, on either side. She was a teenager and she needed a separate world.

"May we go back in the pool?" my older daughter asked.

"Do we have to put our swimsuits back on? They're wet," my younger daughter said.

"No, of course not," I said, as I saw with a shock that my older girl, not yet ten, was showing the first signs of pubescence. Suddenly I was sad, for I saw that I was going to lose my little girls. One day they were going to separate from me.

"The screened porches look like a boat," I said, looking up.

"We used to sleep out there in the summer," my husband said.

"I know," I said.

"But when we did," he said, "it reminded me of how we used to sleep out on the fire escape on hot summer nights when we lived in Brooklyn, before we built this house, when I was little. Everyone would drag their mattresses out on the fire escapes and in the morning you would wake up with all your neighbors all around you on their fire escapes in their pajamas, and it was like being in the garden of Eden."

III. "I am writing to tell you about my journey home."

My Sister Was Just Here

MY SISTER WAS JUST HERE FOR a visit. We had many long talks. She told me about her last visit to Los Angeles. I was unable to go there this year, and I wanted to know how our aunts were. She told me that one day while she was there she took Aunt Lil out to lunch. She is eighty-five now, and blind in one eye, and she gave up driving several years ago. So she asked my sister if she would take her by her old house on Warner Avenue. She had heard that several of the houses surrounding it on that block had been demolished, that high rises were going to be built there. But when they got there, my Aunt Lil's house was the only one on the block that was not still standing. It had been leveled, and all that was left was a couple of boards. But what was most shocking to my sister was how small the lot looked, and how small the hill behind it, this place that loomed so large in our lives.

Now my sister is back in Portland, Oregon, where she

lives. She has written me to tell me about her journey home. "It was so clear," she wrote, "I could look straight down on Lake Shore Drive in Chicago. Lake Michigan is huge. North Dakota looked horrible. There are so many vast spaces in this country. And then the pilot announced that we were passing over Walla Walla, and I was looking down on it." Last night it was late before the children were asleep. I turned out the light, and the wind began to sough in the trees outside our bedroom window. I thought of how my father and I had argued when he was here recently about how the word "sough" was pronounced. He said it rhymed with "bough," and I said it was soft, like "enough."

The Air Hangs Heavy

THE AIR HANGS HEAVY, AND IT is so hot, it is difficult to move. The first time my husband came to my house in Sebastopol there was a heat wave. The temperature was in the nineties. I wore a red sundress and went to the garden to pick strawberries, waiting for him to come. This memory is in the heat, and in our bodies, and today my husband has stayed home so that we could have a day of love. But now the children are home from day camp, and we sit at the table eating rice and vegetables out of bowls. Faces appear in the windows.

It is our friends, the Spectors. They have come to use the lake, and we decide to join them down there when we finish our supper. Clouds have been gathering and the lake is sea green. The children run ahead, and by the time I have set up my chair on the sand they are already half way to the dock which floats a few hundred feet out in the water.

"Why don't we go out in the boat?" my friend Paula asks.

About a year ago, the Spectors brought their old duck boat here and put it on the shore, bottom up with the other row boats. Paula and I went to a hardware store and bought a chain and a lock, and we chained it to a tree. We had visions of spending most summer evenings peacefully rowing around the lake. But we never took the boat out once.

The oars are back at the house, and Paula and I walk back to get them together. I ask her if she is adjusting to the fact that we are moving away yet. Even though we haven't announced this fact to the general congregation yet, I had to tell Paula since our other close friend, Harriet, knows. However, I put off telling her for several months as I kept waiting until I had time alone with her. But she has been extremely busy for the last several months, and we haven't seen much of each other. Nonetheless, she took the news quite hard. "I haven't seen you much in the last few months," she said, "but I always knew you were there."

When we arrive back with the oars, our daughters come running up to us and take the oars out of our hands. We go to inspect the boat. Paula has brought the key to the lock.

But when we find the boat, we are not sure it is really their boat. It is not chained to the tree. "That's it," Paula's husband, Jerome, says. Sacha, their teenage son, begins to turn the boat over. As it comes out of the grass that has grown around it we see that the chain is still on it, but the tree it was once tied to is no longer there.

All the children climb aboard. Paula and I sit in the back. Our husbands watch from the beach. We glide along the shore and the little house I visited last winter with Virginia comes into view. Paula and I begin to talk about whether we are going to dye our hair when we turn gray, and Sacha starts to make fun of us. "Here I am out in the middle of a lake," he says, "and I have to listen to women talk about dying their hair!" What he doesn't realize is that we're *not* talking about the fact that I'm leaving. I'm reminded of the time Paula had a suspicious chest x-ray—how she came to my house and I polished her nails—something neither of us normally does—while we waited for the results of further tests. That time it turned out to be nothing.

The girls dive off the side of the boat, and when they clamber back on they demand to be taken to the island. Paula's lovely daughter Jenny takes the oars. I have always wanted to see the island up close. Last winter, mesmerized by a softly drifting snowfall, Virginia set off to walk there over the ice, but she turned back, frightened, when she was less than half way. She had suddenly remembered that there are springs in the lake.

But now we reach the island in almost no time at all. It is thick with impenetrable growth. The trees come right down to the water, and we are afraid that our boat will become tangled in the roots amongst the lily pads. The island is a mass of growth and decay rising out of the water, but at one time a bridge connected it to the peninsula. At that time there was a mansion on the island, built by one of the original settlers. When he died, however, he willed the island to the town on the condition that the bridge and the house be dismantled stick by stick and stone by stone until nothing remained but the memory.

In All Likelihood

IN ALL LIKELIHOOD WE WILL be packing to leave a full year from now, but there is suddenly the possibility that we will be leaving sooner. This all started when we got wind of a position opening up in San Francisco.

San Francisco is where we would most like to live. At least, we imagine it is where we would most like to live. People at the Seminary have been trying to interest my husband in taking a pulpit in other places, namely, Miami and St. Louis. But I cannot imagine these places.

I go to the encyclopedia and look up Miami. It is much further south than I have imagined. It is in the tropics! I look closer. Children are swinging on swings in their back yards, just as they do everywhere, but even as I watch, a plane comes between me and the children spraying a cloud of insecticide. I turn the page.

Here is a map of the whole country, shaded in differing

ways to show which areas are growing and which not. The whole Northeast is a uniform grey. Florida, however, has stripes, which indicate economic growth. Now it is getting to be night and the lights come on in the millions of new condominiums with their air conditioning blasting. I look over at my dog with his thick shaggy coat. His tongue is hanging out. He shakes his head "no."

So we turn to the entry on St. Louis. We have no family in St. Louis and we know no one who lives there. Of course, we could soon enough meet people. We could soon enough make ties and connections. But it makes me tired even to think about it. I study the map of the city. The city planners have put in a highway which encircles the city, and all the wealth has gone out to the perimeters. The heart of the city has been abandoned. Luckily, my husband has discarded the idea of going here.

Now I open to the entry on San Francisco. The Bay Area is the place where both my husband and I have always felt the most at home. I have lived most of my adult life there. I have friends and relations and connections there. It makes sense that we should be able to go back there.

Still, there is only a remote chance that this will happen. My husband has not been invited for an interview there yet. They have not phoned him yet to determine if they are going to invite him there for an interview. Every time the phone rings now we jump.

We say to each other that if this doesn't work out it will be because the situation wasn't right for us, and we are not going to be disappointed. Still, we have been studying the map to see which route we will take across the country.

Now I look at the map of San Francisco in the encyclopedia until I locate the section of the city where we would live. But even though I have the magnifying glass out now there is only a blank space where our street should be and

I cannot see the treetops on our block or the top of our roof, only the gleaming Pacific which beats against the cliffs where seals bark in the mist.

When We Moved

WHEN WE MOVED TO BEVERLY HILLS I became best friends with a girl my age who lived around the corner, Laura Green. The Greens' house was more luxurious than ours. They had a live-in maid. But unlike our house, which had been designed specifically for us by Joe Jordan, A.I.A., theirs had been built for speculation.

Still, I loved to spend most of my time there, swimming and eating and sleeping over. Unlike our pool, their pool wasn't heated, so sometimes it took our breath away, but there was a waterfall.

The Greens had a tiny room between the living room and the kitchen where Laura and I would always go when no one was looking. I suppose it was a bar, but we called it a candy room because Mrs. Green kept all sorts of elegant candies in there which we would love to sample.

Then we would go down the hall, where the original

Picasso and Matisse drawings were hanging, to Laura's room where we always spent a lot of time dancing in front of her mirrored closet doors. I had no mirror in my own room at home and if I ever wanted to see my bottom half I would have to go into the bathroom, stand on the bathtub, and angle the medicine chest mirror over the sink towards me.

Laura's family was much more formal than mine. We had to be careful not to let her mother catch us barefoot in the living room where there was Italian glass and art books and a grand piano with a bouquet of silk flowers on top of it and a portrait of Laura when she was about eight done in oils. My mother always commented on how beautifully Laura's mother dressed and would never fail to mention, with some disdain, that Laura's father wore spats and went to the opera.

Laura's father was retired, and he speculated on the stock market. But one day he made a bad investment and lost everything, including the house, despite the offer of their cockney maid, Edith, who was by this time quite elderly, to bail them out with her meager life savings.

Shortly after that, Laura's father died of heart failure, and I suppose the two events are connected, though I don't know why they have to be. This all happened while Laura was in the hospital with two broken legs. She had run out between two parked cars after leaving a friend's house in San Francisco. The car that hit her never even saw her. Her long-time boyfriend, whom her parents had never approved of, because he came form a lower social class, perhaps—his father sold tokens in the subway in New York—had dumped her and she was at an impasse in her life.

I am reminded of a story that was on the news last night about a doctor who killed himself and his wife and his daughter with poison injected through intravenous devices. The newscaster reported that the suicide note he had left explained that he had become despondent over financial difficulties, and the picture on the screen was an aerial view of the doctor's house. There were many gables and wings. The house must be very elegant and very large. The doctor was probably going to have to lose this house.

Laura and I

LAURA AND I WERE ROOMMATES when we were in college, during our Sophomore year, when our parents allowed us to move out of the dorms. The only type of apartment they would allow us to move into, however, was a modern one, which we had to share with at least two other girls.

I believe the ethos of the International style was to construct buildings out of inexpensive materials, and this was certainly the case here. Everything about this place was cheap. Perhaps it was because the walls were so thin we could hear through them or because all the units faced each other around an interior court, or perhaps it was because our other roommates ate our food out of the refrigerator and then denied that they had done so—but both Laura and I were soon depressed. We had moved from the dorm to have more privacy, and now we had less.

The other problem was that our building was on fraternity

row. We had disdained to join a sorority—this was the sixties—but the fraternities and sororities enveloped us anyways.

I became friendly with one fraternity boy who rented an apartment two doors down from us. I suppose he needed more privacy than he could get in his fraternity house. I knew we were friends, and not boyfriend and girlfriend, because he never asked me out on a date, and I saw him taking sorority girls in date dresses and corsages past my window and down to the street to his green MG.

Everyone called our building the "zoo." There were iron bars on the balconies in front of each apartment, and in our separate windows we were like animals in cages. One day I was in the fraternity boy's apartment escaping from the sounds of our most hated roommate accompanying herself on the guitar, when suddenly I was drunk. The room was spinning, and he was forcing himself on top of me.

Laura and I moved from that apartment as soon as we could, though our parents protested. They imagined that we were living in decent housing. I couldn't tell them how that building had degraded me.

We Spent a Week

WE SPENT A WEEK ON Martha's Vineyard this August. We came to visit my husband's brother, Jason, and his family. They live here year round.

Their house is in Oak Bluffs, right near where the ferry docks. It is a beautiful grey shingled Victorian, and was once owned by a sea captain. It has views of the water in three directions.

Jason and his wife Injy have two little girls, and with each birth they have expanded the house. On the coffee table in front of the fireplace I found an architect's model of the house with still another addition added on. That was the first news I had that they are going to have another baby.

We slept in the new guest room which was added over the garage, and which connects, via a new bathroom, with the new playroom, where our daughters slept on window seats. But we only stayed there one night. The next day we all moved to their other house on the side of the island at Gay Head.

Jason is a doctor, and on his days off, when he doesn't go off island to his mother's, he likes to get utterly away. That is what the beach house at Gay Head is—a getaway, a retreat. They bought it last year and had it totally remodeled, moving the kitchen to where the living room had been, raising the roof upstairs, and laying beautiful blond wood floors. Now sliding doors lead out to a new deck and the path down to the beach. I had seen the house when they had first bought it, but now it was unrecognizable.

It was very hot during the time we were there, and because my skin is fair, I was unable to spend as much time on the beach as the others. However, from my perch on the couch where I sat reading, I could look out through the glass doors to where the sea sat above the dunes, and I could watch the children coming up the path to the deck where they stepped in the wading pool to rinse their feet before coming in the house. Nonetheless, the house was constantly full of sand. It hurt my bare feet, and I put down my book again and again to pick up the broom and the dust pan. At night, before the children went to bed, I had to shake out their sheets. They had to sit on their mattresses and brush the sand off their feet before swinging them into bed.

I have an old friend from San Francisco, Mitchel Barker, who started coming to Martha's Vineyard for the summer a few years ago. He has become friends with my husband's brother, so Jason invited him for lunch one day when we were there. The last time I had seen him was at my wedding, more than ten years ago. Mitchel is a fine person and a wonderful poet, and I was very interested in seeing him. I was also eager to see his wife, Claudia, as she is an architect, but she had had to fly home to San Francisco a few days before we arrived.

I was also eager to see Mitchel because now the possibility of our moving to San Francisco has become more real. I wanted to ask him about all our mutual connections in the Bay Area so that I could begin to imagine what it might be like to return after ten years.

I was nervous before he arrived, about how he would find me ten years older, no longer able to sit in the sun, but when he came in it was I who was surprised at how he had changed.

He was still handsome and strong, his eyes were still violet, but the years were there, stamped indelibly, around his eyes and under his chin.

"Wipe your feet," my sister-in-law admonished one of our children, coming in, then, from the other direction, but it was hopeless, the sand was filling up the house.

This Summer, Like Last Summer

THIS SUMMER, LIKE LAST SUMMER, the three families, Harriet's, Paula's, and mine, met for dinner in the gazebo behind the house. Last summer, besides us, Paula's mother, who was about to undergo surgery, was there, as well as Harriet's father, who had been staying with her while her mother was in Israel at a convention. At that time I thought to myself that I would arrange the dinner in the gazebo the next year to coincide with my own parents' visit, but it didn't work out that way, and instead, we had Virginia and Bill from across the street as representatives of the older generation, and Paula's friend Pat, an antique dealer, who was visiting from California.

The gazebo is a separate building about thirty feet behind the house. It can only be used in the summer, as it has only screens and no glass. So it is very open and airy feeling. The ceiling is very high with rafters. It is all wood and painted red. Trees enclose it; it feels like a cabin in the woods. There are comfortable chairs and tables there—even two sleeping couches. At our dinner parties, we tend to spread out and clump in little groups. I remember last year that there was a thunder shower, and the sound of the rain on the roof made Harriet's husband Michael exclaim that he thought he was in camp, a child again.

This year there was no rain. We could watch the children swinging in the ash tree just outside. Virginia and Paula talked about gardening and Paula's husband and my husband talked about sports. I suddenly remembered that the first time we had met to eat here was the last time Harriet had seen her father. He had left from here to go home to Far Rockaway, to be there when his wife returned from Israel the next day, and he had died a few days later.

I go to apologize to Harriet. I am afraid it must be painful for her to be brought back here to this place where everything is the same and something is different. But she reassures me that it is okay, it is good for her to be here again, it is good to remember. It is dark now, and the children are chasing fireflies out in the grass.

I think how Harriet's father sat here at the glass table eating hungrily while Paula's mother told him in detail her whole medical history, and when it was time for him to leave, Harriet's husband, Michael, led him out through the dark starry maze of streets where we live to the road which would take him home.

Last Week Harriet Went to the City

LAST WEEK HARRIET WENT TO the city to go to a museum. Before she married Michael, before she had children, before she lived in a house out in the woods, she used to go to museums and galleries all the time. But this was something she felt she had to give up, with not a little regret, in order to have a husband and children and a home in the woods.

Since she is a true New Yorker, she only learned to drive when she had to move out of the city, and the night before her trip to the museum she lay in bed awake, nervous about the drive down to Manhattan. Suddenly she found, to her embarrassment, that she was thinking of a painting of Andrew Wyeth's, "Christina's World." She is too much of a snob, like me, to be a fan of Andrew Wyeth, probably the most popular painter in America, according to the encyclopedia I just consulted. He does not even appear in any of my old college art history texts.

In the painting we see the crippled girl from the back. She is lying in the grass, looking up at her house. Then Harriet remembered the name of the town Wyeth was from, Chadds Ford, Pennsylvania, and thought that this painting must be there, in a museum.

When Harriet met Michael he already owned the land where they later built their house. He engaged her as an architect to design the house before he asked her to become his wife.

The house did not come out exactly as she wished. She imagined it barn-like, and not so monumental. She imagined the stone tower to be like a silo, but from the outside it is like a castle. When I first saw it, I thought of Rapunzel, and Harriet has speculated to me about the possibility that she was unconsciously building a fortress in which to keep herself captive in domesticity, unable to escape back to the realm of pure art.

Still, she is happy in this house, with her children and her dog Pepper cavorting on the blue rug under the tall bank of windows of various sizes which frame the woods outside like paintings in a gallery. Because she is loath to leave her babies her trips to the city have become rare. But last week a large window of babysitting time opened up for her and she suddenly had the time to go and take in the Matisse show at the Modern.

"How was it?" I asked her.

"I couldn't really enjoy it," she said. "I don't like the Modern so much any more since they expanded it."

"I know what you mean," I said.

"It was very crowded," she said. "There was the clack of all these women walking around. And then I found myself in a little room off to one side. The one person who was there was just leaving. I went in and sat down on the bench. There was only one painting in the room, and it was 'Christina's World' by Andrew Wyeth!"

136

"You're kidding!" I said.

"I thought it was in Pennsylvania," she said. "It was so strange to have had that vision of it at home, the night before, and then to find it here, in the middle of the museum, in a room I never knew was there!"

"I bet," I said.

"I sat and looked at it for a long time. I felt I must have been brought there to see something important."

"What did you see?" I asked.

"I saw a woman yearning for her house. Her house is her world. Her house is a whole world. And it's enough."

"Will We Always Live in This House?"

WILL WE ALWAYS LIVE IN THIS house?" my daughter asks me.
"Nobody knows the future," I tell her, although her father
is flying to San Francisco for a job interview in a month.
Before the year is out we will be packing to leave this house
forever.

It bothers me that I must keep a secret from my children,
but we can't tell them until we are ready for the whole congregation to know. Last night I dreamed that I had murdered
a man and had hidden his body in the attic, from which a
stench was beginning to emanate. This man, I think, is my
former husband, still living, unfortunately, near San Francisco. I know I am afraid that if we move there that I will
always be worried that at some time my children will meet
this man and see the horror of their mother's young life. Once,
when we were living in Manhattan, he came there on
business and found our apartment. He came there when I was

at work and the children—then only two and three—were napping. He came just at the time when their father was to wake them and take them to preschool. Later, when he told me what had happened, I cringed when I thought of my babies, of their toussled heads stirring in that house with *his* dark presence, of how they rubbed their eyes with the backs of their hands, unable to dispel the shadows which had come to flood their rooms.

I was grateful that they were too young then to know who they had seen. Nonetheless, I am not going to let this ghost influence our decision, and maybe it would lose its terror in the light of an ordinary day.

I wish I could tell my daughter that we are going to live in this house forever, that her children, as she fantasizes, will also grow up here. I dread the day we will have to tell them the truth. It is getting to be fall now, and many of the trees have bright red splotches on them, as if someone dripped paint on them, like those people who have a streak of white hair because they have experienced a shock. This morning when I walked the dog, the surface of the lake was unbroken, and the red and orange trees on the island reflected out into the water, so that it looked as if the water had been stained with blood.

Last week was the holiday of Sukkot. We have been eating out in the sukkah—a little booth we have built in the yard and decorated with leaves and flowers. My husband, the rabbi, told the congregation that we do that in order to feel closer to God. Out in the sukkah where you can see the stars through the roof there is very little protection from the elements. When we sit in our houses we have an illusion of security—but it is only an illusion.

When we first came to this congregation we stood on the hill and looked at the synagogue. My husband knew he had come to the right place because the building seemed to be all fiery and aglow. Then one autumn he turned and looked the other way—to the west. There was a huge maple tree at the crest of the hill and the leaves were bright red. The tree appeared to be on fire. It was then my husband knew we would leave this place. "I think we're going to go west," he said.

One day we arrived at the synagogue and climbed the hill as usual, but something was missing. The great maple at the crest of the hill was gone. It had been cut down by the chairman of the house committee. He said it had been struck by lightning, but I had trouble believing this as I had been in the habit of observing this tree, and it had seemed undamaged to me. But why he should cut this tree down otherwise I could not guess—certainly not for firewood, as although he had had a fireplace in his house at one time, it had been walled up when he incorporated his family room into his garage so that it would be large enough to house the limousines which were his business. However, I began to worry then about the future of the congregation, which is called *Eitz Chaim*, the Tree of Life.

The other day I heard my daughters making plans with other children about the summer. They assume they will be returning to the same camp they have gone to for the last four years. I can tell that they are happy planning out the future as if nothing will ever change, as if everything will continue on forever just as it has been. The last time my husband and I climbed the hill behind the synagogue I asked him, "What do you see?" He looked at the building and said, "I see a dry brown leaf." We have been reading *Ecclesiastes* in the synagogue because of the holiday, which reminds us that we all will die. "Why do you have to read such depressing stuff at such a beautiful time of year?" one old woman asked. "Look around you!" my husband said, angry then, lifting his arms as out the windows the wind lifted the brown leaves until they whorled up into the sky.

My Daughter Came to Me With a Dream

MY DAUGHTER CAME TO ME WITH a dream she had had the night before. The four of us are walking down the path through the woods to the little house, only the path is narrow, narrower than it is in the waking world.

Last Labor Day Virginia and I went to introduce ourselves to the people who weekend in that house. It was our last chance, Virginia said, before the people closed the house up for the season. She had taken some snapshots of the house as it was last winter in the snow. We were going to confess that we had trespassed there and offer the people the photographs.

As we approached we saw that the little house has been painted a crisp new white. A man and woman came up to greet us. Then the woman took us inside to meet her mother and father, sitting in the screen porch cantilevered over the water.

They were very very old. They accepted our gift graciously, and told us, as we had hoped, that we were welcome to come there with the dogs any time. Then they showed us the house.

It was paneled in a warm dark wood. Patchwork quilts were on the beds in the tiny bedrooms. Through the windows and through the screens of the porch we could see the branches of the weeping willow which held the house in its embrace.

"This table can be extended almost indefinitely," the old woman said, when we stood in the dining room looking out at the water. Bright blue pieces of china stood in the sideboard leaning against the wall. A Beethoven violin concerto played. Above the fireplace were several paintings — all of the little house — painted, the old man explained, by various houseguests — one from the dock, one with a flowering tree in front, one from very far away.

Now that we have permission to trespass, I have taken my husband and children to see the little house. They were enchanted by the road which leads there. It leads directly off the paved road that skirts the lake on which they travel every day, and yet they had never noticed it before. They were delighted with the stone bridge which arches over the stream which runs into the lake beside the house. We came to the dock, and the bench that looks out at the island. The lake had filled with clouds. Only the island separated the water from the cloud-strewn sky above.

Last weekend some children came to visit our girls. After a while they came to tell me they were bored, so I suggested that they take their friends on a walk to the little house. "But I'm not sure I can find my way there," my daughter said.

"Don't worry," I said. "You'll find it."

My husband was down in the city, marrying some people. Because he is a rabbi, he works six days a week, but he always tries to take Monday off, and I also take Monday off to be with him. We never go anywhere or do anything. We just walk the dog together, then eat lunch under the chandelier in the dining room, and take our glass of wine upstairs to bed where we stay for the rest of the day. On Monday we don't answer the phone, but let the machine do it for us. On Mondays we remember how perfect the world is. We are happy then, just to be lying there, our bodies entwined together, in a secret room hidden away from the world.

The phone rings, and the machine takes the message. It is one of my husband's congregants. His mother has just died. My husband will call him back in a few minutes—not just yet. And I think how Monday in this room is like the garden of Eden which still grows at the center of the world, though we think we can never find it, like the road to the little house which has entered our daughter's dream.

Sometimes I Feel

SOMETIMES I FEEL THAT IF I can just observe the lake each day I will learn everything I need to know. Now that so many of the trees which obscure my view of the lake in summer are bare, it has become even more obvious, more present. The geese are gathering along the shore, now. A cold wind ruffles the surface. I can see why Thales thought the basic stuff of the universe was water.

Today when I walked the dog there was a morning fog—unusual here—and when I got to the bottom of the road I found that the lake had been utterly obliterated. My husband has received his plane ticket to his interview in San Francisco in the mail. The possibility of moving there is becoming more concrete.

But how can we return to the Bay Area? Isn't it true that you can't go home again? Like most people, I have a superstitious belief in the veracity of this epigram, though, also like most people, I can't remember a thing about the story. It reminds me of what I said earlier: "I feel the small town was somehow imprinted on my psyche, and I have lived in a series of similarly small towns since I grew up and left my parents' house, looking for home." That is a statement which also sounds true because of the way it is phrased. However, the fact is, I have lived in huge cities, namely, Los Angeles and Manhattan, equally half my life. The truth may be that the home town I am searching for is actually a city. At least, that is what I will believe if we move to San Francisco, because then that will be the way the story goes.

Yesterday My Husband Went With Me

YESTERDAY MY HUSBAND WENT WITH me to pick up our children at their friends' house where they had gone to play after school. He had never been there before, and I had to direct him. "Turn here," I said, when we came around the curve, and we entered the development where these people live.

My husband began to smile. "This is wonderful!" he said. "It's like an amusement park." All the houses in the development were new—and they were all mansions—but each was in a different architectural style—Tudor next to contemporary next to Spanish next to colonial next to French Provincial next to Victorian, etc. It was so odd to see them set next to each other in their new lawns with their twigs of trees that my husband started to laugh, and I joined him.

"You could never be sad if you lived here," he said.

We parked in the horseshoe driveway and went in

146

through the big double doors. "Thank you," he said to our children's friends' mother, when we had gathered our girls and their sweaters and backpacks and were herding them to the car. "Nice house."

The Wind Blows

THE WIND BLOWS, TOSSING DRY purple leaves from the dogwood through the open window. Dry pieces of paper, crumpled messages—but what do they say?

In less than two weeks, my husband will be in San Francisco for his interview. It has been difficult for me to focus on anything else lately. But today is Monday. My husband holds me in his arms under the down comforter. He strokes my head tenderly. All week he has been counseling people whose lives are filled with sorrow. The wind rattles the windows. I am afraid that soon it will rain. I must get up and walk the dog.

Outside, clouds roll in a grey sky. Grey waves peruse the lake. Mrs. McIntyre from across the road is out in an orange jacket. She is stooping to pick up something from the lawn of the house across from her. I think this land belongs to the narrow little house which sits above it, from which the old lady paralyzed with arthritis was taken away one day, but there is nothing on it but two huge trees dressed in burnt orange leaves. Burnt orange leaves cover the lawn, and it is these, I think, that Mrs. McIntyre is gathering.

I've only seen her out once before, though I heard she is a member of the garden club. She is generally disliked in the neighborhood because ever since her divorce she has allowed her house to fall into disrepair and her garden to become so overgrown that her house is almost totally obscured.

The lady from the grey house is crossing the road in a blue coat. She has just gotten her mail. I encounter her perfume as I pass where she just was. I have never met her, but heard how she was robbed last summer of all her jewelry while talking with a neighbor in the house next door. Nevertheless, I have continued to leave my door unlocked.

There is a red wheelchair with a green backpack strapped to its back parked by the front steps of a yellow house. It is small, and I think it must belong to a child. Soon my girls will be home from school.

I stop to marvel at Mrs. Heller's lawn. It is covered with gold leaves. It is a pity that since her husband died she only comes here in the summer. How privileged I am.

I will get my mail before I go back in the house. Some tarpaper from the construction at the Magione house across the street has blown into my yard. Last winter a pipe must have broken there for their driveway became a sheet of ice. They began excavation on it and the excavation and reconstruction of the driveway continued until recently. I remember waking up one night in the summer to the sound of something banging. "What's that?" I asked my husband. "It's the Magiones' driveway," he said.

They have raised tan brick retaining walls on either side of the driveway now, and they have also replaced the roof of the house, another project which went on endlessly, probably because Mrs. Magione doesn't seem to have very much money, not enough to hire anyone efficient and reputable. I am sure her roofers were not reputable because a parcel of ties my husband ordered disappeared out of our mailbox one day when the roofers were there. Now, apparently, they are replacing the windows and the siding. But I wonder if all this is really worth it. The house is very small and plain. Indeed, it has nothing to recommend it. Mrs. Magione has been married at least twice before, and her sons are each from different fathers. One is small and fair and the other large and dark.

I see them playing touch football with some other neighbor boys on the lawn of the house on the corner up on Cromwell. That house is up for sale. It is less than a year since the only son of the people who live there was killed in a car crash. The cheeks of the boys on the lawn are flushed, their bodies rapt. At this moment nothing else exists but the ball.

I Am Waiting

I AM WAITING IN A GRAVEYARD while my husband does an unveiling. I do not usually come with him when he marries or buries people or unveils their headstones, but the graveyard is in Queens, and since we have theater tickets in Manhattan for this afternoon, there is no time for him to drive back home to get me.

This cemetery is very densely populated. I am parked in a forest of headstones: "Abraham Rothchild, beloved father, grandfather, great-grandfather"; "David Gruen, died July 6, 1969, age 53 years"; "Sam Melnick, departed Feb. 7, 1965, always in our hearts."

I can hear someone crying. I remember a dream I had when I was pregnant with our first daughter. In the dream, I am in a courtroom. Seated behind a railing are all my parents—my husband's as well as my own. My death has been decreed, and I ask them if it has to be so. "Yes," they all agree.

"But I am too young!" I protest. "But you will look very old," they reassure me. "You will die of cancer in Berkeley in twenty-five years."

I sit cross-legged in a red robe on a cold stone floor. Through the small window in the stone wall I can glimpse the barren mountainside and the thin pale sky. I am sifting the dust at my feet. There is nothing that I want, nothing that I need.

Needless to say, when I woke my husband, who believes that God speaks through dreams, he reassured me that I had only dreamed this because I was pregnant, because now that I was about to become a mother my life had become more precious. I didn't believe him, and when we moved to New York, far away from Berkeley, I was somewhat relieved.

And now it seems fairly likely that we will be going back. My husband has returned from his interview in San Francisco full of enthusiasm. Since they still have to interview several other candidates, we won't know for sure for several months, but he feels this is our destiny, and so do I. There is no point in trying to avoid what is meant to be. And for me, also, there is the idea that I will be going home.

My husband, on the other hand, is confused about where home is. He was raised in New York, but came into himself in California. And we have been living in New York again all these years.

There was so much about the Bay Area he hadn't remembered—the salt flats at the edge of the Bay, the smell of eucalyptus, all the succulents. He felt like a recovering amnesiac, unable to remember how to get from here to there, the road unfolding before him like a band of memory.

While he was being driven down Nineteenth Avenue, suddenly Stonestown appeared. He had not thought of it one moment since last he had seen it, yet it was the most familiar thing. Stonestown is a shopping center next to a high-rise housing development which has an exact twin in Los

Angeles, near the house on Genesee. It shocked me the first time I saw it up north.

My husband feels he did well at his interviews. However, there was one question he had difficulty answering. They wanted to know why he wanted to leave where he was. Indeed, we have been happy here. Not that there haven't been problems. When we arrived, the synagogue was losing members and had an inadequate school. During my husband's tenure, however, the membership has doubled. He has totally revamped the school. The odd thing is, the synagogue in San Francisco also has been losing members and also has a school which is in trouble. My husband wonders if his experience here was meant to prepare him for what is needed there.

My husband did not know anyone in the congregation in San Francisco before he went there, but, as it turned out, we are not totally unconnected. Indeed, there was a man there who had known my husband's father. He had lived in Woodridge, the little town in the Catskills where my husband's father grew up. In fact, this man's best friend had been my husband's uncle, the one who died in a plane crash over Florida during World War II, the one my husband is named for.

I, also, have a connection to the congregation in San Francisco. "I met a very nice man here," my husband said over the phone. "His name is Dan Zuckerman."

"He's my cousin," I said.

Dan Zuckerman was married to my mother's first cousin, Beatrice. But Beatrice died in childbirth with their second child. Those children must be about my age now.

There is a black and white photo of Beatrice, her lovely brown hair in a pompadour, in front of the house on Genesee. I think she is holding my sister, a baby then. The bay window of the living room is behind her, obscured by a large hibiscus bush. There are blossoms on the bush, and it is possible that they are just about to bloom.

Both my husband and I are anxious, on edge, awaiting the final word. We are eager to set out on that road where all that lies behind approaches, grows nearer, as we get closer to the end.

I Was Relieved

I WAS RELIEVED TO SEE A picture of Friz Freleng, the creator of
Bugs Bunny, in the paper the other day. He was here in New
York because they have renamed one of the streets "Bugs
Bunny Way." I was surprised, and yet delighted, to see him
whole and intact, after what happened.

It happened when I was about ten. I was friends with his
daughter, Hope, a pretty little blond girl, like a little Tweety
Bird, which he also created. Hope invited me to sleep over
at her house. I had my reservations, because I always had
reservations about sleeping in a stranger's house. All houses
outside of my own were strange, full of unfamiliar odors and
corridors leading to unknown, and, therefore, dangerous
places. To sleep in such a place was to expose one's
vulnerability, or to lie awake in a night which was infinitely
long.

Hope's house was old, a Spanish-style duplex with

wrought iron bars over the windows and thick walls which rendered the interior dark and muffled every sound. It was filled with heavy dark furniture. Hope's mother was pretty, little and blond. She spoke in a soft voice and disappeared down the hall.

Hope had an idea: We would rearrange the furniture in her room. Or maybe it was my idea. Probably it was.

The furniture was heavy and large. It was not easy for us to shift the massive chest or the four-poster bed. The rug bunched. It took us the better part of the afternoon. Hope's mother came to the door to call us in to dinner. I saw her jaw drop. Then I saw the final effect of our efforts—the chest blocking the door, the bed now inaccessible from either direction.

We ate at the dark wood table. I lowered my eyes to my lap. There was a gouge in the edge of the table in front of me. How had that happened? I was wearing my favorite belt—the one with metal reindeer sticking out from it. I prayed then that no one would notice.

I'm not sure how I endured the rest of the time I spent there. I never saw Hope again after that. Shortly afterwards, to my secret relief, we moved away to Beverly Hills, where I thought that I had escaped scot-free. But now I see that I carried with me the heavy furniture from Hope's house, and that it has been inside me ever since.

To Get to My Parents' House

To get to my parents' house in Beverly Hills you turn off of Beverly Drive onto Laurel, which leads to Carolyn Way. Coming or going you must travel on Laurel. There is a house on Laurel which I passed every day I lived there which evoked in me a sense of emptiness and longing because it was to me so beautiful, so perfectly a house, archetypal, rendering flimsy and insubstantial all the other houses in my experience, most especially the one in which I was made to live.

It is a Cape Cod house, with real deciduous trees in front. It clearly belonged to a tradition. It spoke to me of belonging, although in actuality it stuck out like a sore thumb on this road of Hawaiian-style houses and the new Greek temple house which was later erected next door.

Now I see that my love for this house was only an instance of a familial wish to belong, to rise in social class to

157

a level where one could simply be, and not question one's ability to participate in reality.

When I first moved to Beverly Hills I was courted by the girls in the seventh grade. For a while, I spent a lot of time with a classically cute blond girl, Susan Kramer. She lived on Roxbury Drive in a huge pink house with a high pink plaster wall enclosing the yard, the long rectangular pool and the cabanas.

The pool was dark and deep. Susan's parents were very old and left her pretty much alone. She had her own wing of the house, and when I spent the night, I took a bath with her in her private bath and slept with her in her double bed.

As is the case in many of those old Beverly Hills mansions, the walls of Susan's house were crumbling, but I didn't care. I followed her up the stairs, past the little room where her parents sat, their drinks frozen in their hands.

The Apartment

THE APARTMENT LAURA AND I moved to after we left the zoo was what my father called a fire-trap. It was upstairs, with only one exit. My father had a very literal idea of safety, but this was of little concern to either Laura or me. We were quite willing, being young, to jump out the window if need be.

We liked it because it was extremely quiet, far away from the excesses of fraternity row. It was on Dwight Way, below Telegraph, and faced north, so it was dark and cool, permeated by a filtered green light. There was only one bedroom, which Laura and I shared, and we pooled our clothes.

In the living room there was a large green overstuffed chair that looked like it had been there since the thirties, and a small Formica table with two metal chairs, but otherwise the room was poor and bare. We each acquired a proletarian boyfriend.

Mine was named Ken Kaufman. He was slightly

depressed. His father was a truck driver. He came from El Monte, outside of Los Angeles.

Once, when I was home in Beverly Hills for a vacation, I borrowed my sister's car and, telling everyone I was going over to Laura's house around the corner, I went out on the freeway for the first time alone and drove myself to El Monte. Ken's house seemed to be made out of cardboard. In the back room was his sister, retarded or demented, I wasn't sure. That was the period when I involved myself in political causes. I was arrested in the Free Speech Movement and participated in sit-ins in Jack London Square to protest hiring practices that discriminated against Blacks.

When Laura's parents came in their big black car to move her out at the end of the semester I was surprised at their coolness towards me. Certainly my own parents had been horrified at my activities, but I thought that Laura's parents, because they cared for art, would be on the side of social justice and idealism. But they seemed to think I was a bad influence on their daughter.

The next year, Laura and I didn't live together. She decided to transfer to an art school, and moved in with some other art students in Oakland. One of them, Phoebe, had an affair with Laura's proletarian boyfriend, Tim. The other was a quiet girl who later joined the S.L.A. and participated in the abduction of Patty Hearst.

160

The Next Year I Lived

THE NEXT YEAR I LIVED WITH two young women who had been the girlfriends of our proletarian boyfriends before we came along. I was no longer seeing Ken, and Linda and Sheila were happy enough to share the rent with me.

We found an apartment on Dwight Way, above Telegraph, in a place that was called "Zinzandel Court." It was owned by Cal and later torn down so that the University could build a parking lot there. However, this was prevented when the citizens declared the ground "People's Park" and planted gardens there. Now, I believe, the Berkeley Art Museum is there, as well as the Pacific Film Archive, which my husband and I each have separate fond memories of, recently dredged up in our new meditation on life in the Bay Area.

Zinzandel Court was shaped in a U. Our apartment, the only one to have two stories, was in the rear, past a giant prickly pear cactus.

My room must have been the dining room. It had a

Murphy bed which folded down from the wall. I hung a bead curtain in front of an alcove I used as a dressing room.

You had to go through my bedroom to get to the kitchen, and through Linda's, which was the living room, to get to the stairs which led to the bathroom and Sheila's room, but we all got along there because, after all, we each had rooms of our own.

Since it was on the ground floor and there was a back door, my father couldn't call it a fire trap, but he almost queered the deal anyway, because of the refrigerator, which was dirty and old, and he made the university replace it with an equally dirty and old refrigerator.

Zinzandel Court was pink. The sun shone past the prickly pear through the leaded glass windows and sparkled on the beads of my curtain. The rooms glowed. I had ceased all my political activities, having realized that I had little talent in this direction. I still, however, believed I could change the world, but it would have to be by another way.

I began to write. I heard the guitar of the dark handsome poet in the apartment next door and saw the flowers on the cactus open.

Because It Has Become Cold

BECAUSE IT HAS BECOME COLD the house has become more cluttered. We have shut the glass door to the little room. It is not heated and has become unusable. We have put the down comforters on the beds upstairs and they seem to fill the rooms. Then there is the unceasing traffic of mail on the white table, dog toys on the floor, newspapers, art supplies left out, laundry overflowing the basket, cosmetics obscuring the bathroom and appliances devouring the kitchen. If one lives in a cottage, and this is a cottage, because it is cozy and because it is small, one must constantly simplify the number of one's objects and possessions until the only ones that remain are those both essential and beautiful.

However, this is a job that is never done; the force for clutter in the universe is too powerful. Outside the window now the trees are all twiggy sticks, also messy after the summer's shimmering mass of featureless green, the full flesh which covered the bones so well I never remembered they were there.

This Sunday my husband and I went to the holiday party of the county's self-help cancer support group. They have asked my husband to be their spiritual counselor. The party was held in a night club called "The Class of '57." The owner had lost his wife to cancer two years before and had donated the space.

It was dark inside, and smoky, yet I could still see that the faces of the guests were pasty. A tape of saxophone music unwound around the smoke while huge football players fell to earth on a giant t.v. screen. Then these were both turned off. It was time to give out the awards.

An award was given to the little seamstress who sewed turbans for them and to the owner of the hair prosthesis shop who treated them with humanity and gave them their wigs at cost. A plaque was awarded to commemorate the bravery of a twenty-six year old woman who had died that year. Her husband came up to accept it, and their three little children were introduced. There was the announcement of a donation presented by a cancer victim's widow to fulfill her husband's dying wish—to send children with cancer whose course would not turn back to Disney. My husband walked to the front to accept his award for volunteering. Over his head the neon words "rock 'n roll" glowed in the gloom made gloomier still by the fact that we all knew that outside it was still light.

There was barely enough light left to walk the dog when we got home. The neighborhood looked messy to me, the garbage cans left out, the twiggy branches revealing every flaw on every house. Since last week was Thanksgiving, the Christmas decorations have started to appear, although all the Hallowe'en decorations haven't yet been removed. In front of a very poor house where there was only dirt where the grass should be was an orange plastic garbage bag with a pumpkin face only half filled with leaves now, so that it looked like a face that had caved in, next to a tall plastic snowman. Lining the walkway to the house were the same plastic tin soldiers that didn't light up that were there last year. It depressed me to see them again.

I started heading downhill towards the lake and home. It was almost completely dark now. The hills on the other side of the lake were a featureless dark mass. The lake had captured all the light left in the world. It floated before me, and the rest of the world fell back. No longer water, it seemed to be light. It was not light, it was emptiness, and it comforted me.

IV. The door is closed, and the voices
start up again.

My Grandmother Lived in One Room

MY GRANDMOTHER LIVED IN ONE room during the time I was growing up. It was an apartment near Wilshire Boulevard, and she would spend her days in the department stores, looking at the things and sitting on the round ottomans positioned by the gleaming glass doors. My grandfather had died the year I was born, and I think she gave up on life then. I would have been named "William" after him had I been a boy. "Another girl!" she said with disdain when I appeared. At least, that is how the family story goes.

During the time I knew her, my grandmother had very few possessions. Her studio apartment came with its own impersonal furniture—a scratchy couch and a chair, a blond coffee table, and a Murphy bed which came down from the wall but was always up when my mother brought me for our weekly half-hour visit. I don't know what happened to all the things she must have had before she was widowed, the pots and pans and china and crystal and blankets and lamps and rugs and cookie jars, though I think there was a cookie jar in her tiny kitchenette, and a sewing box and two or three glasses turned upside down. My mother told me they had had a grand piano when she was a child, and Chinese rugs, but these had been taken away one day during the Depression. Still, they must have kept drawers and tables and rolling pins. Where did all these things go? Where are they now?

All my grandmother had in her tiny studio apartment was a tiny refrigerator and a hot plate. She ate most of her meals out alone at Dupar's restaurant or Van de Kamp's cafeteria. On her wall was one picture—of her—done in pastels when she was a beautiful young woman. In one of her drawers where her undergarments were carefully folded was a switch of her hair, cut off in her youth, and this I always asked to hold.

There were Venetian blinds on the windows, and through the slits I could see the apartment building of a man who had asked my grandmother out and had brought her perfume, but whom she had disdained to see again. In her tiny dressing-room/kitchenette were several other bottles of expensive perfume, each from a man whom she had disdained to see again. These bottles displayed their amber liquid, but I never smelled their scents; they were never opened.

A few years ago my grandmother's younger sister, my great-aunt Estelle, moved from Oakland to Connecticut to be near her only son, and we visited her there. We found her living like my grandmother, in one furnished room. Also like my grandmother, she had brought with her very few personal objects, and in the bathroom there were bottles and bottles of expensive perfume, set out on display. None of them had been opened. I never saw her again, for she died the next year of heart failure.

My mother tells me that my grandmother came to every one of my birthday parties, but I have no real memory of her at any of them. When I turned sixteen my mother made a party for me at an expensive restaurant. I dressed in a silk flowered dress and we drove to my grandmother's apartment in my mother's white Cadillac. My grandmother had never learned to drive, and we were coming to pick her up.

But she didn't answer when we knocked. My mother had a key, and she opened the door, but it only opened a few inches. The chain was on. Through the slit I could see that the metal Murphy bed was down from the wall. A form was writhing in the white sheets.

My grandmother had taken an overdose of sleeping pills. My mother went to the manager's office to telephone the police and the ambulance which would come and take her away, knocking her knees together, to a hospital where her stomach would be pumped and her life would be saved.

While my mother was gone, I stood transfixed, looking through the narrow slit in the door, where my grandmother's boney white hands grasped the metal frame of the bedstead. Her body twisted in torture on the bed as if her life was being cruelly constricted inside, and it was trying to get out.

It Is So Cold

IT IS SO COLD TODAY THAT MY face hurt when I went out to walk the dog. I pulled my hat over my face, but then it was difficult to see where I was going. The ground is brittle and hard with borders of frozen snow leftover from last week's storm, and the sky is a continuous leaden grey. When I come back in the house, the chill and this leaden feeling follow me in. We are still waiting to find out what is going to happen — where we are going. This weekend we had a visit from two men from the search committee of the synagogue in San Francisco, but still we won't know their final decision for another month, or possibly two. In the meanwhile, my husband is applying to other places, though it is difficult for me to believe in the reality of alternative places.

I'm really not sure why the men came here from San Francisco. Perhaps it was to see my husband again — to reassure themselves that the person they met when he went out there was not an illusion. This I can almost understand. When I first met him, I wanted to be pinched—to see if I was dreaming. It is possible, of course, that they wanted to come to see what *I* was like, but if that were the case, they could have had me out there. What is most likely, I think, is that they wanted to see our house. I always want to see people's houses after I get to know them, for the inside of a person's house is the three-dimensional aspect of the inside of that person.

So before the gentlemen from San Francisco arrived, I cleaned out each closet. I didn't want them to find any of our skeletons.

"How many bedrooms do you have here?" they asked me, one after the other.

"This house is really inadequate," I confessed, blushing.

They sat at the dining room table before they left, and I fed them lunch. My husband described to them how to get to the airport. "You have to get on 280," he said.

"But there's a 280 in San Francisco," one gentleman said.

"It's a short cut," I said. "Just get on 280 and you will be able to avoid the plane altogether." They had come here to prove to us the reality of the place they came from, but had ended up characters in a dream.

That night, after they were gone, the children took out the video camera their aunt and uncle had just given us. My husband has never wanted to have a video camera, because shortly before his father died there was a tape made of a family party in which he appears. It hurts my husband to look at this tape. This electronic image is not his father, he says.

The girls decided to make a video letter and send it to their grandma and grandpa in California. However, they were not used to using the camera and took a lot of shots of the ceiling and floor. The ceiling is made up of acoustic squares and the floor fake tile. Neither one do I care to look at. This is not how I view my house inside my head. They did their photography at night, and the interior of the house seemed murky. As we reviewed the tape before sending it off, I wanted to deny that this was in fact present reality—this house inside this box with its areas of darkness.

For Most of Her Life

For MOST OF HER LIFE, MY husband's sister has lived close
to her mother. In fact, she has lived most of her married
life back in Usonia, just over the hill from the house
where she grew up, where her mother still lives. Her
husband is a corporate lawyer, and commutes to Manhattan, just the way her father commuted for most of her
life. Like her mother, Carol has never worked, but has
spent her life taking care of her family, everyone else who
needs her, and her house. Her house is a thing of beauty in glass and warm wood with slate floors. She has furnished it with white carpets and couches like the white
clothes she wears which set off her golden beauty. Carol's
life has always seemed comfortingly stable to me, so it
came as a shock last week when we heard that her husband's company has decided to move to Florida within
nine months. Her husband will try to find another job

175

here so that they won't have to move, but the climate for this isn't good right now, and his chances are slim. Yet how can Carol leave her mother? I suppose it is theoretically possible that my mother-in-law will also move to Florida, but we all know she will never leave her house.

My own sister, similarly, has always been tightly involved with our mother. Unlike me, she lived at home all through college. She lived at home for her first few years as a teacher, until the minute she got married. I was glad when she moved with her husband to Portland, Oregon, because she had a chance, then, to live her own life. And, indeed, they moved into an old two-story house with a basement, but after a while they sold that house to move into my sister's dreamhouse. It looked uncannily like my parents' house in Beverly Hills. Indeed, it might be the only house in Oregon with a pink rock roof.

Recently a friend was here visiting from Montreal and he asked why I didn't put the storm windows down. He said I could save quite a bit on my heating bill if I did. "But," I said, "then I wouldn't be able to open the windows." Then I explained to him that I leave a window open in my bedroom at all times, whether the temperature is zero degrees or eighty. This I do ostensibly for the cat, who climbs up the dogwood, then jumps on the roof of the portico and from there to the window. However, this window would be open even if we didn't have a cat. If I sleep with all the windows closed I will have bad dreams.

In one of the first bad dreams I had as a young child my house has been taken over by witches. There are no rooms, but only hallways painted red and orange in which a witch has trapped me.

Earlier than this is my first dream, the dream which antedates memory. I am in an underground passage. The walls are rough, and so low that I have to stoop or crawl. It is lit

176

with a dull red light, like a darkroom where images coalesce in dark water. It is so hot that I can barely breath, and I feel that I am going to suffocate.

We, Like Everyone Else

WE, LIKE EVERYONE ELSE IN the world, are waiting to see if there is going to be a war. A war seems inevitable, yet unreal, as we have been waiting for almost six months for it to happen. However, I have been waiting even longer to find out if our family is going to move to San Francisco. The fate of the world hangs by a thread now, and all I can think about is where home will be in six months.

This weekend, Harriet's husband took their daughter and went to Florida to visit his parents. Harriet decided to stay home with their little son because traveling is too complicated now with the children at this age. She had plans to visit many people while they were gone, but as it happened, a snow storm came and shut her in the house. She called me late on Saturday night because she had worked herself into a state. Her dog had been out for many hours, and though she called and called at the door, he wouldn't come home.

She couldn't go to sleep, could do nothing but wait for him to appear. Of course, she was waiting for the Gulf crisis to come to a head on some abstract level also, but in real life she was waiting for her little dog Pepper to come home.

This Waiting to See

THIS WAITING TO SEE WHAT IS going to happen is torture, but it occurs to us that this may be the happiest time of our lives. My husband seems to have grown younger. He claims he feels like a teenager, not a man in his forties. The future is open and full of possibilities. We are living on the edge, and life is full of passionate intensity.

I am excited also at the possibility that the place we are moving to will turn out to be home. Tomorrow we are going furniture shopping, although we have no idea what we are furnishing.

We had a big snowstorm this weekend, and it is interesting for me to notice how everyone's spirits lift, including my own, as soon as it starts to snow. I am sad when I think that we may move to San Francisco, out of the snow forever, that this pure white miracle will be consigned to memory in my children's hearts as they disappear into the fog.

However, in a week my husband is going to Vermont for an interview, and should we go there, our lives would very quickly fill up with snow.

Right now I am waiting outside a movie theater where my children have gone to a birthday party. It is Sunday morning and the sun shines, reflecting off the white snow covering the fields and piled up along the side of the road. Ice glistens in the bare twiggy branches of the trees as it melts.

I'm not sure how I feel about Vermont, as I have never been there. Everyone says it is quite beautiful, but there is something about the cold that frightens me. As we drove here to this theater this morning we passed the goose pond which is in the center of our town. Children skate there in the winter. Now it is covered so completely by a blanket of snow you wouldn't even guess it was there. But last week some children were skating there and two boys fell through the ice. A woman who a moment before had been describing to her chidren how to save someone from the ice borrowed a hockey stick, got someone to hold on to her ankles, and lay down on her belly over the ice, extending the stick so the boys could reach it and be pulled out. So she saved their lives.

My girls wanted to know why the boys couldn't just walk out of the pond, since it's quite shallow. Then their father told them that the danger was not drowning, but freezing, that the water beneath the ice freezes you and you cannot move. So you freeze to death.

On the way home, the woman who had saved the boys remembered that as she lay on the ice reaching the hockey stick toward the boys she could hear the ice cracking beneath her. She remembered this sound and a sob came out of the crack, because she knew she was alive.

The First Time We Went

THE FIRST TIME WE WENT TO Jerusalem together as a family we went for a summer so that my husband could study in a special program. All the students were being housed in dormitories in a place called Kfar Goldstein. They asked us if we would be able to live there, since we had a toddler and a baby six weeks old, and we told them that of course we could. We could live in one room.

The first night we slept in that room the sun came up at about four-thirty in the morning. A bird flew in the window and nested in my husband's straw hat. The flimsy crib that had been provided for us wobbled and threatened to collapse with our baby inside. Our toddler took off down the hall towards the open stone stairs. "This won't do," I told my husband. "Don't worry, I'll fix it," he said.

They found us a large room on the ground floor in another, uninhabited area of the compound. The walls were covered with graffiti and there was rubble outside the door. Down the hall was a lavatory with many sinks and toilets, most of which were stopped up with standing water. I made my husband accompany me there when I needed to go. When he was in class, I crouched on my cot with my feet off the floor and my babies in my arms.

"This won't do," I told my husband. "I'm working on it," he said.

We lived this way for ten days, and then he found us an apartment.

It was the first apartment he found, and we could only have it for a month. He had had to talk the agent into renting it to us as she wasn't supposed to rent it to anyone with children. Together they went and rolled up the rugs and put as many of the antiques and art objects as they could into one of the bedrooms and locked the door. Then a taxi came and brought us and all our luggage and Georgette, the Moroccan teenager we had hired to help out, over to the apartment.

It was the most luxurious place I ever lived. I felt we deserved it, after what we had been through. It was very large and sunny, but cool in the heat of the day. There were several balconies, and the breeze blew in. Every day Georgette went shopping for food and paper diapers. She was an accomplished cook. Her soups and her cheesecake were especially delicious. In the afternoons she took the girls and me on the bus to the bank or the old city. Because of the language problem and because of the babies, I was practically helpless, and I let Georgette do all the cooking and cleaning while I took care of the girls. When they were asleep at night I would bathe with my head on the pillow in the tub. In contrast to the apartment we rented a few years later in Talpiyot Mizrach, this apartment had endless hot water.

One Saturday afternoon when we were resting together on our bed we saw a trickle of water start down the wall. As we watched it, it grew. "I'll take care of it as soon as the sun sets," my husband said, and as soon as it was dark he opened the high cupboard in the hall which housed a water tank. He stood on a stool and peered in, then climbed into the cupboard to take a closer look. "I think all I need to do is tighten this valve," he said, as we waited below. Then suddenly a torrent of hot water came pouring down from the cupboard and the lights went out.

"Are you all right?" I screamed in the dark, as my husband came climbing out of the cupboard.

"Waters come down! Waters come down!" our big girl repeated, over and over.

My husband was not injured, but the water continued to pour into the apartment. He ran all over the building, knocking on doors, looking for help. Finally, he found a woman on the top floor who led him up on the roof where they located the solar tank belonging to our apartment and turned off the water. By this time, some friends had come over and helped me hold the baby and the candles and start to push the water out with the giant squeegee used for cleaning the floor. "Waters come down!" my big girl said.

Meanwhile, on the roof, the woman who was assisting my husband fell and broke her collarbone. The police had to come and carry her off the roof. She had been in the midst of packing to leave for a sabbatical in America, but now she would be unable to travel. Later, my husband went to visit her several times to thank her and to apologize, but she never seemed pleased to see him.

We left that luxurious apartment when the month was out and moved into one perhaps more appropriate to us in the old Catamon district. This had a simple pine table, high ceilings and white-washed walls. There were wrought iron bars on the windows and shutters which we closed in the heat of the day. When we lay in bed in the early morning we could hear the Arab women calling in the streets, selling the prickly pears they carried in baskets on their heads.

Georgette was still cooking for us, but I was getting tired of not taking care of my family myself. When we found she was stealing from us, we fired her and I started buying the food. I never knew what I was buying, and once the breaded fish I thought I was buying turned out to be chicken.

I am thinking of all this now because the war with its chaos and destruction, terror and distrust, has begun. I never met either of the people who owned these apartments where we lived that summer. I can't pretend I really know what it is like to be them, though I drank from their cups and slept on their sheets. I am reconstructing those apartments today because a force has been unleashed in the world which is trying to obliterate them. I reconstruct in an effort to keep them standing, their roofs and walls and interiors intact.

It Is Deathly Quiet

IT IS DEATHLY QUIET. SNOW frosts the trees and the windows, icicles hang from the eaves. The sun shines, illuminating the hollow interior of this room. The world seems empty. There is no one on the road. No car goes by. No one is home next door or across the road or around the corner. This morning my husband went to Vermont for a preliminary interview. We have heard from a source that San Francisco is still very interested. Meanwhile, the Seminary is pressuring my husband to apply for a position in Chicago. These three places, Vermont, Chicago, and San Francisco, are so different from one another that they seem to contradict each other. Each of these possibilities cancels the other two out. The house is more empty with my husband gone to Vermont than it is when he is only over at the synagogue. It is empty though I am inside.

186

I Go Out to Walk

I GO OUT TO WALK THE DOG. The temperature must be in the
low fifties; the black snow is melting. The brook babbles and
a small brown bird flies low across the road in front of me
chirping for all the world as if this were spring and not the
end of January. The Canada geese fly in their v's overhead,
honking convivially, as if cormorants in the Persian Gulf were
not today fatally covered in oil. I see they are doing some
construction at the villa around the corner. They have had
a new baby; they expect the world to continue.

Many houses are now displaying American flags. Yellow
ribbons have joined the Christmas wreaths, plastic tin
soldiers, and deflated pumpkin garbage bags. I am glad to be
outside. Last week was so cold that I was unable to walk the
dog. I thought my bones would crack. So I put him on the
line. My husband put on his long johns and went to Vermont
for his interview.

He liked it there very well, but has decided to turn them down. I am glad, perhaps because in my imagination in the long Vermont winter there is only this bone-cracking cold, there is none of this thawing and freezing which we have here. "We have learned to respect the winter," my friend who has moved to Montreal said when he was here, putting hats and gloves and scarves on his children before taking them out to the car. I do not like the idea of not being able to go out easily, without endless bundling and without pain. I am afraid of being made to stay in.

Last night, watching the news of the war, we were told of the hardened shells where Saddam Hussein's aircraft have been hiding, of the underground bunkers where his elite troops are waiting and of the fifty odd underground bunkers he has all over the country where he can wait out even a nuclear attack. We were even shown a floor plan of one. It was huge, full of endless rooms in a catacomb configuration. Under the sand, deep in the cold earth, he remains, death laughing from the grave.

The First Place I Lived Alone

THE FIRST PLACE I LIVED ALONE was in an apartment on Walnut Street in Berkeley my senior year. I rented this apartment with Laura, but she was never there. This was only the address she gave her parents; she was actually living with her boyfriend. It was a pleasant apartment with walnut-stained lintels and glass French doors hiding the Murphy bed in the front room where I slept. There was a pretty gilt-framed mirror in the dark hall where I could only get a dim view of myself on my way out to class. I did not like being alone.

This was also the first time I had lived on the north side of the campus. It was quieter here, more serious, more mature. I was on the second floor, and had a bay window which opened to admit the blue light of evening and the smell of coffee roasting at Mr. Peet's coffee shop below. Once I made coffee in an aluminum percolator on the little stove, but I forgot about it for several weeks, and when I went to make coffee the next time I found green mold growing on the grounds. I could not bear to look at it, and threw the whole thing in the trash, pot and all. Clearly, I still knew very little about the practical world.

What I did know was my walk to and from the campus through the grey world on the edge of rain where nasturtiums loomed and eucalyptus let out its pungent scent and dropped its seeds and leaves in my path. Each building on campus was built deliberately in a different architectural style. All of history was here, everything there was to know. Wheeler Hall, where the English Department was housed, was one of my favorite buildings, of course, with its broad staircases that I would climb breathless to my professors' offices under their blue copper mansard roofs. The dull shine of the brown floors and walls, the high ceilings, the heavy lintels, the solid doors and glass transoms, the hanging white light fixtures— all filled me with purpose and longing, and I would walk back to my apartment, past one perfect cottage after another in which I wished I lived.

I slept in the Murphy bed in the room with the bay window, but there was another, smaller bedroom in the back which looked out at the garden. This room was very green, very leafy, darker than mine. Laura eventually sublet it to a friend of hers, Dotty, who closed herself inside. Her boyfriend had broken up with her, and now she withdrew into solitude, and I very rarely saw her.

I was spending most of my time with one of my teachers, a graduate student, the man I later married. But one night when he was sleeping next to me on the Murphy bed I felt something awful flying around our heads. He jumped up and turned on the light, and it hung upside down over the window. It was a bat, and it filled me with horror. The window had admitted this creature in the evening when it hung open, perhaps as a warning to me that there was something wrong with this relationship I was more and more deeply involved in. However, now I was even more afraid to be alone, and made plans to live with this man when I began graduate school in the fall.

Nonetheless, I was sad to leave that apartment at the end of the year, sad to be leaving this part of my life. So when I was packing I removed the gilt-edged mirror from the wall in the hall and put in into one of my boxes marked for home. In the act of stealing it, it caught my reflection just as I was then—setting off on the wrong path in life.

It was wrong of me to steal it, but I was young and trying to hold on to something which would continue from one place I lived to the next, and indeed, that mirror has been with me ever since. It is here, now, on my white dresser in my room upstairs.

It is, as it happens, not the only thing I stole. I also have a quilt that belongs to Laura. She had two of these identical on her twin beds in Beverly Hills, and I always slept under one when I slept over. We used these quilts on our beds when we went away to college. When we stopped living together I still had her quilt; I never returned it. It was now full of holes and couldn't be mended. Eventually I sewed it between two sheets, rose chintz, and tied it down with tufts of yarn. My husband and I sleep under it now on Friday nights, when we are at the synagogue. To look at it you would never guess what it contains—those times we laughed all night in Laura's childhood room. And in the mirror is my white face, before I reached to take it from the wall.

I Am Entering Once

I AM ENTERING ONCE AGAIN EACH place where I have lived. I walk into each corner and pass through each room. I walk down each hallway trying to get home. The wind comes and bangs shut the door behind me. Ahead, another door is pushed open. When one door closes, another door opens. I follow each path up each set of steps to each doorway, opening inward. It is dark, and I turn on the light. It is light, and I open the shades. I can hear my own footsteps overhead, then my feet on the basement steps. I am in the attic, trying to close the window. There are mice and birds in the house, which the cat has brought in. There are cats and dogs and guinea pigs and fish and a white rabbit with grey above its nose. There are children in the house, one of which I was. I open the drawers, and the doors to the closets, and then I close them, because to make a door open you must first shut another door. Time is passing quickly and I am in a hurry to get home. So I shut each door behind me carefully, and they make a hollow sound as they close. The latches catch, they shudder in their frames.

My Husband Felt Shaky

MY HUSBAND FELT SHAKY AFTER he called Vermont to turn down their offer. The same day he learned that because of seniority rules he might not be allowed to apply for the place in Chicago. "But you don't want to go there, anyway," I said. "You want to go to San Francisco."

"But San Francisco hasn't called in weeks," my husband said. "What if San Francisco falls through?"

"When one door closes, another door opens," I said. "To make one door open you must first close the other doors," I said.

"The doors are closed," he said, as the phone rang.

It was one of the gentlemen from San Francisco. He was calling to say that they would be calling us again in less than two weeks to arrange a date for my husband and me to fly out for another weekend. He couldn't say anything official, but he wanted my husband to read between the lines and have in mind when they called back the terms that would be suitable to him were San Francisco to give him an offer.

"I'm not sure, but I think I got the job," my husband said, when he got off the phone. "It's not exactly in the bag, but it's very close to the bag."

"But you think it's going to happen?" I asked.

"I always thought it was going to happen," he said. "From the moment I heard about this position I thought it was our destiny. But it's in God's hands. If it doesn't work out, then it wasn't meant to be. If I didn't believe that, then I would have no business being in this business."

"But you put in your request?" I asked.

"Oh, yes," he said. "He knows.

I began to think about our impending visit to San Francisco. If everything works out, we will move out there in July. We will rent a house for my husband's first contract, for the first two or three years, and then, if his contract is renewed, and things work out, we will buy a house.

That slot on applications marked "permanent address" has always mystified me.

When we go out to San Francisco in a few weeks or a month it will probably be too early to rent a house, but I will walk in concentric circles on the streets surrounding the synagogue wondering which house is going to be mine. When I first met my husband we took a trip to New York so I could meet his family. A friend of ours happened to be giving a lecture in the living room of a Columbia professor's apartment on Riverside Drive in the city, and we drove down to see him. But we got there too early, so we went for a walk around the neighborhood, down Broadway, under the scaffolding erected on most of the buildings. Years later I learned that bits and pieces of these buildings, most of which belong to Columbia, had been falling off them, wounding or killing the people below, and they all have had to undergo extensive repair. These repair procedures disturb the mice, and they run into

195

the apartments, under the counters and along the wainscotting. As we walked, we passed Papyrus Books, where I was later to shop, and the West End Bar and Grill, a famous jazz club on the corner of Broadway at West 113th Street. We walked down West 113th Street towards Riverside, past the building where we were later to live my husband's first two years of rabbinical school. The idea of coming to the Seminary had not yet occurred to us, nor would it until several years later, when my husband's increasing need to study Judaism made it necessary for us to leave Sebastopol. At first we thought we would move to San Francisco, and we put our order in for that, and perhaps that order is at last about to be filled, but there was no seminary in San Francisco, so my husband came to New York for an interview.

They said, "Come right away," and within two weeks we were in Jerusalem for a summer of intensive Hebrew, and, by September, ensconced in our apartment on West 113th Street between Broadway and Riverside. Then we remembered how once we had walked down this street together, thinking to kill time, and how we had said to each other, "I wonder what it would be like to live here, to shop in that store and walk in that door." Somebody, clearly, was listening.

"I Have Misunderstood"

I HAVE MISUNDERSTOOD GEORGETTE," Harriet told me on the phone the other day. Georgette Pallor is an acquaintance of mine, but a closer friend of Harriet's since their husbands share a medical practice. I knew that Harriet was fond of Georgette and rather hurt when the Pallors never followed through with their vague promise to have Harriet design a house for them. Recently they had taken her to see a house they were thinking of buying instead.

It was in a development, a lavish one, one where each house is different, like the lands in Disneyland, from Tudor to Mediterranean to Greek to Futurist. The one they had selected was Victorian with all the curlicues. But all the curlicues were made out of aluminum, and the house itself, like all the houses in the development, was blown out of proportion. It looked like it had been inflated with helium.

197

"What do you mean you misunderstood Georgette?" I asked.

"Well, she and Lenny have just moved to a house they are renting. They sold their old house and thought they would just rent while they decided what they wanted to do, whether to build on the property they have or buy another house."

"So they didn't buy the Victorian house?" I asked.

"No, they want to buy the house they're renting. But they may have lost their chance. Georgette is really upset. She was crying on the phone."

"What's it like?" I asked.

"It's not in a development," Harriet said. "It's an old old house, out in Campbell Hall. I was over there yesterday. It's right by a railroad track, and the train goes by and toots once a day. She said it reminded her of her father. She said her father used to work for the railroad, and when he died, she came out of the hospital and a train was going by, very slowly, and the engineer was waving to her. I really misunderstood her.

"All her furniture—she has all this old antique furniture—looks just right in this house, too. It's the same furniture she had in her old house, but I never really noticed it there. I never really 'saw' her before I saw her in this house."

"What's the house like?" I asked.

"You'll have to see it for yourself," Harriet said. "Why don't you go over to see her? I'm sure she'd love to give you a house tour."

"Maybe I will," I said.

That Saturday I found myself standing next to Georgette's husband, Lenny, after services. Georgette wasn't there. She had stayed home.

"I heard you're trying to buy a house in Campbell Hall," I said.

"We're trying, but I don't think it's going to happen," he said. "We made an offer, but it was contingent upon getting an engineer's report. After all, it's a very old house. There might be asbestos. We know there's asbestos in the basement. Who knows what there is. But these other people offered the owner the same money and they didn't ask for an engineer's report. So they took *their* offer."

"Why don't you offer more?" I suggested.

"We did!" Lenny said. "We offered them twenty thousand dollars more. But the other people put a binder on the house. There's nothing we can do. All we can hope for is that the other buyers won't be able to sell their old house. But actually, they've already sold it. All we can hope for is that the people who bought it won't be able to qualify for a loan."

"Oh, dear," I said.

"But I've been photographing the molding in the house in Campbell Hall so if we have to move we can recreate it. We can build it again on the property we own. We can recreate it down to the smallest detail, but without the asbestos. It's just so perfect for our family."

"I'm going to come visit Georgette," I said.

"She'd like that," Lenny said.

I went the following week. I had no idea where Campbell Hall was. It turned out to be in the middle of nowhere—a crossroads with one or two stores. Georgette's house was right in the center, right by the railroad tracks. It was big and white with green trim. Georgette's feelings for this house had reminded me of how I felt about my own house, which is also white with green trim, though tiny—irrationally in love with a place I had just happened into, a place filled with what would be taken to be defects by anybody else.

In many ways, I could see, Georgette's house was a nice old place. It was sunny, the ceilings were high, and the fireplace in the dining room was very pretty. Massive molding framed the doors. This was the molding that Lenny was busy photographing so that he could recreate its specific vanilla embellishment. It reminded me of something: the molding on the doorway in the picture of the dreamhouse one could live in if one won the Publisher's Weekly sweepstakes.

However, to my mind there was a lot about that house that wasn't so wonderful. The kitchen work space was extremely tiny and cramped. "Less to clean up!" Georgette said lovingly.

There had been some inappropriate additions during the fifites and sixties. Georgette, smiling, pointed out a sixties kitchen fixture hanging in one of the upstairs bedrooms. Clearly, this had charmed her. "I put the table here in front of the door so no one will walk out on the porch," she said, gesturing towards the rotten porch.

"I'm using this back porch as a closet as there aren't enough closets here," she said, delighted.

"Of course, this house costs a fortune to heat," she said, smiling. "Today the weather is mild, but last week I couldn't get the house warm enough. We all had to wear long underwear."

We had ended up at the kitchen table looking out through the window broken into many sections, probably in the fifties. Georgette had placed colored glass bottles on the window ledges. Through the window, I could see the little store across the road. "How did you and Lenny meet?" I asked Georgette.

"Oh, actually we met at an airport. In Chicago. I was flying home to Buffalo, and Lenny was on his way there to start his residency. Actually, he proposed to me on the plane."

"Oh, you had love at first sight!" I said. "So did we!"

"When I tell most people they think we're crazy," Georgette said. "No one believes in it unless they've had it."

"I know," I said, "but I don't believe in the other kind."

"I Was on My Way"

I WAS ON MY WAY TO A CONFERENCE out on Long Island," Louis said. We were standing together talking after services. Louis is a psychologist who works with troubled children. "Suddenly I saw this exit sign and a strong force pulled me off the expressway," he said. "It was a sign leading to the town where I had been born and where I had spent the first five years of my life, never to return.

"I stopped at a service station to ask directions. Across the road was the A & P which I remembered. Actually, it was no longer an A & P, but a structure in the shape of the A & P. I drove to the street where my first house was, and as I got closer I became flooded with emotions. All these feelings started to come back."

"What kind of feelings?" I asked.

"All these good feelings of being loved and nurtured," Louis said. "I had a very happy childhood. I felt I was really getting in touch with the child in myself. I'm very aware of the child in myself. I go to a lot of workshops where I try to get in touch with and nurture that little guy."

"How nice," I said. "But what about the house? Did you see the house?"

"This was the most amazing thing," Louis said. "I found the house and the people who live there now were standing outside saying goodbye to their guests. I told them who I was and they couldn't have been nicer. I just kept feeling all these feelings. It was so incredible. The people who lived next door were outside too. They were the same people who lived there when I lived there, and they remembered me! They remembered one time when I fell off my bike. It was so incredible."

"But what was the house like? What kind of a house was it?" I asked.

"A Cape Cod. I think it was a Cape Cod. It was very small. All on one level. There wasn't any upstairs."

"Then it couldn't have been a Cape Cod," I said. "What was it like inside?"

"Oh, I didn't go inside," Louis said.

"Why not?" I asked.

"I don't know," Louis said. "The whole experience was so powerful. I had such powerful feelings."

"Yes, but what were they?" I asked.

It Snowed

IT SNOWED, PERHAPS FOR THE last time in my life. I remember painting snow scenes with dabs of white poster paint on black construction paper when I was a child in California, before I had ever been in a snowstorm. All snowstorms I have been in since have reference to these paintings where, for me, the primary reality of snow falling exists. This snow was very wet, and piled up on the bare branches. The sun came out the next day and glared through the windows. It reflected off the wet white paint that covered the world. How unnaturally bright it was.

It began to melt. Rain came, and helped. Crocuses appeared suddenly. Robins hopped on the lawn. Now birdsong fills the morning air. The trees are poised to release their leaves. Already, this morning, I saw a weeping willow with new narrow yellow leaves. The willow is the first tree to get its leaves and the last to lose them.

It is two weeks now since my husband and I returned from San Francisco. We will be moving there in three months. The deal is done. I had forgotten how beautiful it was, forgotten all the pastel houses. I think it's possible that we will be happy there. I don't know where we will live. People there are looking for a place for us to rent. I can't help but worry. Rentals, especially to people with a dog, are few and dear.

The day before we went to San Francisco my husband got an offer from Chicago, where he had been for an interview the previous week. This offer was so good that I wouldn't have had to work. It was so good that we would have gotten out of debt. It came with a large five bedroom house with a fenced yard for the dog. The people in Chicago were shocked when my husband chose San Francisco over them. To them, of course, Chicago is home.

When we first returned from San Francisco we were very happy. But I had trouble readjusting to the time. Every day I felt more tired. I had a strong desire to sleep, and beneath this I felt a gnawing anxiety and depression, maybe because I am worried about finding a house and a job, and maybe because I'm sad to leave my friends. But perhaps this is just what is called "depression before spring." The world is waking up now after its long winter sleep. Soon there will be a rush of blossoming, of burgeoning. A force stronger than thought will push out the grass. Everything will come into leaf. Everything will begin to move at an accelerated pace. Soon, everything will be transformed. The world opens one eye and sees that this is coming. Then it stretches, wishing, like me, to stay in bed just a little longer.

I Awake From a Dream

I AWAKE FROM A DREAM. THEY have found for us two square
rooms in San Francisco. Why should we take this when we
can commute from our big house full of staircases and cor-
ners? My husband awakens, on the other hand, knowing with
a certainy that they will find us a charming spacious place
that we will love. "Stop worrying about it," he says. "It's done."

I peer out the window of the train on my way to work,
passing towns full of pleasant houses, yellow ribbons flying in
their trees, umbilical cords pulling their loved ones home.

When I return my husband has a smile on his face. They
have called from San Francisco and they have indeed found
a place for us to rent close enough to the synagogue so we
will be able to walk there in three minutes.

I am in shock. He begins to describe it to me. It was built
in 1916, and is quite spacious with high ceilings. There are
hardwood floors, and there is wainscotting, a fireplace, a

sunroom, a back yard, and a bathtub on legs. Had we put in our order we could not have found a place more perfect for us. Then I think how, in my way, I did put my order in.

This is not the first time a place has been found for us while we were far away. Both our apartments in Manhattan were found for us when we were in Israel different years, and we rented our apartment in Israel sight unseen when we were in New York. Most people, when they move somewhere, go around looking at many places to live in and then choose one. However, it does not bother me that we are not actually choosing this place. I am sure that it is the place that is meant for us.

I did not choose to fall in love with my husband, but I loved him from the moment I saw him. He was meant for me. Similarly, from the first moment we heard about the situation in San Francisco we felt it was to be. We felt compelled to go there—propelled there by a force so strong even our children feel it and are ready to go.

I look at our new street on the map. Through the tops of the trees I can see myself heading out the door and down the front steps with my dog. We decide to turn right, and go the block and a half to the little park marked in green. In the middle of the park is a blue lake, with a broken line encircling it. I am not sure how large the lake is, or how long it takes us to circumambulate it, but when we have done so, we find our street once again, and, finally, we wend our way home.

Right Before Candle Lighting

RIGHT BEFORE CANDLE LIGHTING on the first night of Pesach Harriet calls to wish me a good holiday. She tells me that in preparing for the holiday—cleaning the house and removing the *hametz*, putting away the regular dishes and pots and bringing out those used only on Passover, covering the stovetop and counters with foil and the tables with three layers of cloths—in the act of doing all this she has been brought very close to her mother and her grandmother, who went through these same motions year after year. I, also, have gone through this procedure, not only at my house, where we will spend the intermediate days of the holiday, but also at our apartment in the synagogue, where we will spend the first two and the last two days of the week. I have also had to *kasher* the big synagogue kitchen, as I needed to use it to cook for my seders. One thing I will not miss when we are in San Francisco is this moving back and forth from the house to the synagogue apartment for the sabbath and those holidays when we don't drive. It seems that no sooner have I unpacked then it is time to pack up again. I feel I am on a treadmill, and I can't make any progress. So I am not so cheerful as Harriet, but rather tired and grumpy.

I am also a little jealous of Harriet. My mother and grandmother, after all, never *kashered* their houses for Passover. But, of course, my great-grandmothers did, and their mothers before them. Their world, I suddenly see, is here now, in what is no longer my ordinary kitchen, but a kind of eternal Passover kitchen with covered surfaces. It is a kitchen from which the dishes and kettles and pots of this time and place have disappeared, replaced by the Passover dishes and utensils which reappear for one week every year and then are carefully sealed away. It is my ordinary kitchen, limited by time and place, with the eternal Passover kitchen superimposed upon it.

I go out into the large school room which for the past five years we have used for our seders because it is larger than the dining room in the apartment. I have arranged three tables in a square and covered them with a patchwork of white cloths. I have covered the blackboard at one end with the lace tablecloth my mother gave me on her last visit. It was a gift to her fifty-two years ago at her wedding. Over the blackboard at the other end of the room I have draped a table cloth with blue flowers which I took from my husband's grandmother's apartment after she had died. I place the silver candle sticks my mother bought in Mexico one year when we went there on a family vacation on the table. These sat on the dining room sideboard in Beverly Hills until she gave them to me last year. They are not traditional sabbath and holiday candlesticks, but I remember how beautiful I thought they were when she first bought them, and I treasure them now.

My mother-in-law arrives with the flowers she has brought for the centerpiece, and the other guests begin to arrive—the guests we have had seders with all the years we have been here—our friends Jerome and Paula Spector, with their lovely teenage daughter, Jenny, and their son Sacha home from his second year at Yale; our friends Henry and Zamira Galler, with their daughter J.J. home from Brandeis and their son Lawrence home from the navy where he is an officer. We also have invited this year a young man named Sam, so we are fourteen at table.

The Gallers and the Spectors have been with us every year, but I also feel the presence of the other people who have sat with us at this square table for other seders—Elena and her daughter Anna, the Marshalls, the Fincks and the Horns, my friend Shoshonna who is in Israel now and, last year, two families of Russian immigrants having their first Passover seder in freedom.

The seder commences with its familiar rituals and readings and long discussions. Every word is said as it is said every year; we atomize the text at such length that it seems we will never get to the meal; then, suddenly, it is time to eat the matzo. My husband, the rabbi, tell us that we must eat the matzo for four minutes in silence, and abruptly the buzz of discussion stops and we are tasting the bread of affliction once again. I look across the table at my friend Paula sitting opposite me. Like me, she is wearing a black linen jacket as it is rather cool in the school room. I feel like I am looking in a mirror, or, more accurately, that I am locked inside a mirror and I cannot speak. Now that my voice is stopped tears come to my eyes. Paula reaches up to wipe her eyes. This is the last seder we will spend together.

The four minutes are up and the buzz of discussion recommences, the voices covering over the raw reality in the room. We eat, we laugh, and we sing, and finally, it is time to open the door for Elijah.

When I was a child, this was always my favorite part of the seder, for it always seemed to me as we stood with the door open that something powerful entered the room. My husband suggests that we stand for a few minutes silently, remembering all those who are no longer here, before we sing "Eliahu Hanavi," and as we do I see my mother-in-law is silently weeping, and I remember a séder nine years ago that we had with her in our apartment in New York. My husband's father was in the hospital then, and he died a few weeks later.

Each year we have been in the East, my husband's mother has come to spend one night of Passover with us. The other night she always goes to her daughter's house, where the rest of the family gathers. But next year we will be in San Francisco, and Carol will be in Florida. I look around the table at all the young people, all about to disappear off into their lives. But the purpose of this night is to relive what it was to be a slave and what it is to be free. The candles burn, and the wine sparkles in Elijah's cup, and I know there is no end to this moment. This room is not limited by its physical dimensions. And then the door is closed, and the voices start up again.

Printed November 1991 in Santa Barbara & Ann
Arbor for the Black Sparrow Press by Mackintosh
Typography & Edwards Brothers Inc. Text set in
Trump by Words Worth. Design by Barbara Martin.
This edition is published in paper wrappers;
there are 200 hardcover trade copies;
125 hardcover copies have been numbered & signed
by the author; & 26 lettered copies have been
handbound in boards by Earle Gray, each with
an original drawing by Sherril Jaffe.

Photo: Neah Fisher

Sherril Jaffe lives in San Francisco with her husband, Rabbi Alan Lew, and their two children, Hannah and Malka.